TAG ALONG

TAG ALONG

TOM RYAN

ORCA BOOK PUBLISHERS

Library and Archives Canada Cataloguing in Publication

Ryan, Tom, 1977-
Tag along / Tom Ryan.

Issued also in electronic format.
ISBN 978-1-4598-0297-1

I. Title.
PS8635.Y359T35 2013   jc813'.6   C2013-901917-0

First published in the United States, 2013
Library of Congress Control Number: 2013935376

Summary: Friendships are forged on prom night, when four teens help each other
through disappointment, near-arrest, parental interference and panic attacks.

*Orca Book Publishers is dedicated to preserving the environment and
has printed this book on Forest Stewardship Council® certified paper.*

Orca Book Publishers gratefully acknowledges the support for its publishing
programs provided by the following agencies: the Government of Canada through
the Canada Book Fund and the Canada Council for the Arts, and the Province of British
Columbia through the BC Arts Council and the Book Publishing Tax Credit.

Design by Teresa Bubela
Background cover image by Andrew Wooldridge; photo strip images by (top to bottom):
Masterfile, Getty (Peter Augustin), Getty (Enamul Hoque), and Masterfile
Author photo by Andrew Sargeant

ORCA BOOK PUBLISHERS
PO Box 5626, Stn. B
Victoria, BC Canada
V8R 6S4

ORCA BOOK PUBLISHERS
PO Box 468
Custer, WA USA
98240-0468

www.orcabook.com
Printed and bound in Canada.

16 15 14 13 • 4 3 2 1

For my parents, who taught me to live a creative life.

ANDREA

Newton's third law of motion says that every action has an equal and opposite reaction.

For instance, when I drop six feet from the roof of my garage, the third law tells me that my butt will hit the ground with as much force as the ground will hit my butt. When I land, it feels as if the ground has come out the winner, but you can't argue with science. Equal and opposite. Thanks, Newton.

I groan and roll over to lie flat on my back. I stay there for a minute, staring up through the soft leafy canopy of the maple tree that marks the edge of our yard. Then I struggle to my feet, brush off the back of my shorts and stand for a moment, trying to figure out what to do. There's not much *to* do other than get out of here, so I hurry down the street before one of my parents happens to look out the window.

If you'd told me a month ago that I would go to these lengths to get out of the house, all for the sake of prom, I wouldn't have believed you. Sure, I was planning to go to prom, but only because that's what you're supposed to do. I'm not into clothes the way my best friend Bethanne is, and I think dancing is weird. I'll never understand what compels people to lose control and shake around like a bunch of maniacs.

Then the Justin Sanchez thing happened.

Justin's been in most of my advanced-level classes since ninth grade, and I guess you could say I have a bit of a crush on him. He's quiet and a bit geeky, but he's really smart and definitely cute, and until a few weeks ago, I didn't think he knew I existed, let alone knew my name.

It's not like he's some ladies' man or whatever—as far as I know, he's never even gone out with a girl—it's just that we've never really spoken to each other. Then a few weeks ago I had a dentist appointment and missed my afternoon classes. That night Bethanne called me, practically hyperventilating.

"Guess what?" she said. "Justin was asking about you today!" She's the only person who knows I'm into him.

"What do you mean?" I asked. "What did he say?"

"He said, *Where's Andrea?* and I told him you were at the dentist. Isn't that awesome?"

"Is that it?" I asked her.

"It's a start!" she said. It didn't really sound like much, but the more I thought about it, the more I began to see that she had a point. He'd gone from not acknowledging my existence to noticing my absence. That had to count for something.

"You've got to make a move," she continued. "The ball's in your court."

"What ball?" I asked her.

"Andrea," she said. "He came up to me out of nowhere and asked where you were. That's the ball."

"Well, shouldn't I wait for him to talk to me or something?"

"No," she said. "Justin Sanchez has no game. If you want something to happen, you have to make it happen."

Tonight is the prom, which is obviously as good a place as any to make my move. When I woke up this morning, I was genuinely excited. Bethanne had helped me find a great dress, red with black trim and a flared skirt that ends just below the knee. I had an appointment to get my hair done and a plan to go to Bethanne's house so we could get ready together. Most of all, I had a good feeling about me and Justin. I'm not talking about fate or destiny, just a positive reading of the facts as I knew them.

Of course, the facts as I knew them this morning have changed. As of right now: I'm not going to be talking to Justin tonight; I'm not going to be dancing with Justin tonight; I'm definitely not going to be making out with

Justin tonight. As a matter of fact, I won't even see Justin tonight, because I'm not going to be at the prom.

Everything might have worked out just fine if Bethanne hadn't convinced me that we should get some alcohol for the dance. I feel the same way about drinking as I do about dancing—why do it?—but Bethanne wouldn't let up, so I asked my brother Brad if he'd buy some for us.

Brad doesn't live with us anymore. He's taking a graphic-design program at the community college in the city, and he has an apartment with his girlfriend, Janelle, who is awesome. She's very loud and funny, and she's studying theater at university.

"Yeah, no sweat," he said when I asked him about the booze. "Just promise that you'll keep an eye on Bethanne. I don't want to be hauled off to jail because she gets wasted and streaks the prom."

About a week ago, he picked up the sugary wine cooler that Bethanne requested, and I hid it in my closet. Probably not the best idea.

This afternoon, I borrowed Mom's car for my hair appointment. When I got home, she was sitting in the living room waiting for me, the bottle of Raspberry Comet Cooler in front of her on the coffee table. I could tell right away that this wouldn't end well.

"Where did you get this, Andrea?" she asked.

"What were you doing in my closet?"

"Answer my question," she said.

"I stood in the parking lot outside the liquor store until some old man agreed to buy it for me," I told her.

"I have a hard time believing that," she said. No kidding.

"Well, that's what happened." I wasn't going to rat out Brad. I wouldn't put it past her to call the cops on him.

"You can lose the attitude, young lady," she said.

I swear, seventeen years on earth and I'd never done anything to piss her off. It was like she'd been waiting all this time for something to happen, as if she just needed to prove to herself that I'm going to end up like Brad, who barely made it through high school. Never mind that I've got six years of straight-A report cards under my belt.

I tried reasoning with her, although I knew it wouldn't work. "Mom, please just pour it down the sink and forget about it. I won't drink—I promise."

"Oh, I know you won't drink," she said, in her patented *I know what's best for the world* voice. "You're grounded for a month, Andrea. You can forget about the prom."

So that's how I ended up sitting in my room this afternoon, staring at my dress drooping on a hanger in my closet like a sad, headless puppet. After a while, Mom knocked on the door and, without waiting for me to answer, stuck her head in.

"Honey?" When I didn't answer, she pushed open the door and just stood there, staring at me. I didn't look at her.

"Pouting isn't going to help you," she said. Her voice softened a bit. "You sure you don't want something to eat? You feeling okay?"

"Are you kidding?" I said. "Of course I'm not okay. I'm grounded."

"Andrea, choices come with consequences. I don't want you to end up doing something stupid. I'm not going to do this all over again."

"You mean like with Brad?" I asked her. "Mom, you know that's not fair. Brad almost flunked out of school."

"Exactly," she said.

"Exactly what?" I asked. "I'm on the honor roll. How perfect do you want me to be?"

"I don't want you to be perfect," she said. "I want you to be safe."

"Safe," I repeated. "I'm locked up in my room for my own personal safety. Got it. Can you at least leave me alone, so I can be safe in private?"

"What are you going to do?" she asked. "Just sit in here and brood?"

"Mom. Please leave me alone."

"Okay, fine, but please come out and eat something if you get hungry. I'll put a plate of supper in the fridge for you."

When she closed the door, I gave her the finger.

I got off my bed and pulled my dress out of the closet. I stood in front of the mirror and held the dress in front of me, staring at myself, noticing how different I looked with my hair up off my neck, admiring the color of the fabric against my skin, imagining what I would have looked like if I'd actually had the chance to dress up.

Not to be vain or anything, but I thought I would have looked awesome, and I was pretty sure Justin would have thought so too.

I shoved the dress back into the closet and slammed the door, then pulled the bobby pins out of my hair and shook it out so that it hung down to my shoulders again.

It's not like I planned it, but once the idea hit me, my mind was already made up. I threw on a hoodie and grabbed my wallet and cell phone.

Then, before I had time to talk myself out of it, I jumped out the window.

PAUL

When Lannie Freston and I first started going out last summer, I felt like I'd won the lottery.

I'm still not sure how it happened. I was just minding my own business at the beach with my buddies Jerry and Ahmed when all of a sudden Lannie and her girls showed up and spread their towels a few feet away from us. In no time at all, she was asking me to put lotion on her back. I sure as hell didn't put up a fight.

It was as easy and as quick as that. Suddenly I was her boyfriend. She told me later that she'd been eyeing me up for a while and that sitting near me at the beach was no accident. It was like she'd just flipped through the yearbook and decided that I was the one she wanted to go out with. *And on the seventh day, Lannie looked at Paul and said, 'Let him be mine,' and it was so.*

Obviously, I wasn't going to complain. Lannie's one of the hottest girls in Granite Ridge. She's smart, athletic, popular and even has her own car. We spent the rest of the summer going to the beach, driving into the city and hanging out with her friends. Every long summer night ended with us parked somewhere secluded, doing what you do when you're sixteen and Lannie Freston is your girlfriend.

Then the summer ended. We went back to school, and just like that, because I was going out with Lannie, I was at the top of the heap. I know it sounds arrogant, but it's true. I'm not going to lie—it felt good to walk down the hallway and know that people were turning to look at us. Wishing they *were* us. For someone who had spent most of his life trying to fly under the radar, I was surprised at how much I liked the attention.

A lot of things changed when we started going out. For one thing, I didn't see nearly as much of Jerry and Ahmed anymore, except at school. I just didn't have much free time anymore. Whenever there were other people around, it was usually Lannie's best friend, Darrah, and her boyfriend, Ryan Penner. I'd never really known Penner all that well, but now I was hanging out with him all the time. Penner's pretty cool, I guess. Besides, it was easiest to just go with the flow.

So anyway, Lannie had been talking about prom for months. She wanted to go all out. She bought an expensive dress and took me into the city to order a tux, even though we're juniors and only seniors wear tuxes.

She said she wanted us to make a splash. In those last couple of weeks before the big night, it seemed like every conversation we had was about prom. What kind of corsage I should buy her, where we'd get our pictures taken, what restaurant I should take her to beforehand.

I went along with everything—rented the tux, got a haircut, made dinner reservations at the fancy restaurant she suggested. I went along with all of it, because it was no secret how important all this stuff was to her. But yesterday, after we picked up my tux, something shifted. I got home and hung it on the closet door and then sat on my bed and stared at it.

That's when I felt it, for the first time in years.

At first it came on pretty soft, as if someone was carefully wrapping his fingers around my brain and gently squeezing. It was definitely there though—I could tell the minute it started. I lay down on the bed for a few minutes, taking slow deep breaths, and by the time Mom called me for supper, I felt okay.

I had hoped that was the end of it. But today I woke up super early to the sound of my phone vibrating on my bedside table. I reached over and groped for it. It was a typically early text from Lannie.

Rise and Shine! Big Day!

I groaned and checked the time. Seven thirty AM.

This time it came on instantly, and instead of fingers lightly pressing on my brain, it felt like a belt was cinched so tight inside my head that my thoughts were going to suffocate. My heart started to race and my skin got cold. I snapped off the ringer, tossed the phone onto the floor and pulled the covers over my head. I tried to remember my breathing exercises from a few years ago, and eventually I managed to calm myself down a little bit. It still wasn't good though. My head was spinning and buzzing, and every slight movement made me want to puke. I couldn't imagine getting out of bed.

I don't know how long I stayed like that, but at some point Mom knocked on my door.

"Lannie's on the phone!" she called from the hallway.

She knocked again, and when I didn't answer, she stuck her head into my room.

"Paul, Lannie's on the phone. She says she's been trying to reach you all morning." I didn't say anything. I couldn't. "Paul?"

I pulled the covers off my head, and when she saw my face, she raised an eyebrow at me.

"Is it back?"

I could only nod.

"Is it bad?"

I nodded again.

"Does Lannie know about this?"

I shook my head.

"Don't worry, sweetie," she said. "I'll take care of it."

She went downstairs, and after a minute I could hear her talking on the phone. I managed to sit up and swing my legs sideways, and somehow I made it down the stairs.

I stopped, leaning against the doorway to the kitchen, and watched as she finished her conversation.

"Okay, dear," she was saying. "I should probably get off the phone and see if Paul needs anything. Okay, I will. Yes, definitely."

She hung up and looked at me with a concerned expression I hadn't seen since I was maybe thirteen.

"Is she pissed?" I asked.

"She isn't a happy camper," Mom said. "She'll live though. You okay?"

"I guess so," I said, shrugging.

"Oh, sweetie," she said, walking over to reach up and hug me. Not an easy task considering that I'm six foot three and she's tiny. "I'm so sorry that your prom is ruined this way."

"What did you tell her?" I asked.

"I told her you're sick, and that you've been in the bathroom with diarrhea all morning."

"Mom!"

"Trust me," she said. "She didn't ask any more questions after that."

I went back upstairs to my room and picked up my phone from where I'd tossed it. There were already three new texts from Lannie. I didn't bother reading them. I already knew the gist. I dropped onto the bed, lay flat on my back, closed my eyes and concentrated on my breathing. The thing about a panic attack is that once you get your breathing under control, you're halfway home.

I started to feel a lot better, but I knew it could come back without much warning.

I couldn't even think about the prom right then. I just lay there, breathing deeply. In and out. In and out. I felt my mind steadily relaxing, tension rising from my body like steam.

* * *

When I wake up, my alarm clock tells me I've been sleeping for hours. I feel better, a lot better, although a bit groggy. It's six o'clock, which means we've missed our dinner reservation and Lannie is probably on her way to Terry Polish's house for the pre-party.

I glance across the room at the tuxedo and an uncomfortable shiver goes down my spine. I haul my ass out of bed and shove the tux into my closet so I don't have to look at it.

A movement across the street catches my eye, and I look out the window in time to see Andrea Feingold climbing out of her bedroom window and onto the roof of her garage. Weird.

I watch as she scrambles over the edge and hangs there before dropping to the ground. She lies there for a minute, staring at the sky, then gets up and turns back to glance at her house before running away down the sidewalk. I've known Andrea for a long time, and I've never seen her act like this. I wonder where the hell she's going.

I go downstairs and out the sliding glass doors to the back deck.

Dad is home from work, and he and Mom are relaxing at the patio table. My brothers are wrestling in the backyard. "We've already eaten," she says. "We didn't want to disturb you." She slides a plate with a couple of burgers and some potato salad across the table at me.

"So, you're missing prom, eh?" Dad asks as I tuck into my food.

I nod, my mouth full.

"Can't say I blame you," he says. "I always hated that kind of thing when I was in school."

"Do you think I can borrow your truck?" I ask him once I've finished eating.

"You sure that's a good idea?" Mom asks.

"I'm fine," I say. "I just need to get out of the house for a little while. Get my mind off things."

She looks like she wants to say something else, but she keeps it to herself.

I expect my dad to tell me to take Mom's Corolla, like he usually does. Instead, he reaches into his pocket and tosses me his keys.

"Sweet, thanks!" I say.

"Be careful where you show your face," says Mom. "I've convinced Lannie that you're on death's door. She probably wouldn't enjoy seeing you bumming around town."

Yeah, no shit, I think. Funny thing is, now that I know I'm not going to prom after all, I feel like a million bucks.

CANDACE

I wasn't even planning on going out, but my father has been watching TV and drinking beer since noon, and my grandmother is busy in the kitchen. I figure if I stick around it will just turn into another episode of *My Depressed Dad!* and the last thing I want to do on Friday night is sit around Gee-ma's sad little bungalow helping my forty-five-year-old father regain his self-esteem. Then what would we do on Saturday, right?

I decide to hit the road. I grab my backpack from my room and I'm trying to sneak down the stairs and out through the front porch when Dad yells for me. I consider ignoring him and bolting, but instead I roll my eyes and go into the living room.

My grandmother's house is like a time capsule— wood paneling, tacky green furniture from the seventies, thick orange carpet, a gigantic TV in a wooden cabinet. There's even a heavy glass ashtray on the coffee table, even though nobody around here has smoked since before I was born. It's like time has stood still since Jimmy Carter was president.

The most depressing thing is that it's always perfectly neat and tidy. Gee-ma vacuums every day, and the place smells like lemon furniture polish. I imagine her getting up every morning and going through the exact same routine. The only thing that's changed is that now it's my dad flopped on the couch instead of my grandpa.

It's only six o'clock, but the drapes, heavy and brown with a swirly beige pattern, are drawn tight against the sun. The TV is blaring, and all the lamps are turned off. It might as well be midnight.

"Hey," I say, standing in the doorway.

"Where're you going?" asks Dad, his eyes not even leaving the TV.

"Just out. Might go see a movie or something."

"You're not going to get into any trouble, are you?" asks Dad, somehow managing to pull his eyes away from the TV and look at me.

"No." I'm not in the mood to get into this.

"Well, don't forget to say goodnight to your grandmother," he says. "And don't stay out too late." As if he cares. As if he isn't going to lumber into his room at nine and hibernate until almost noon tomorrow.

I walk into the kitchen, where Gee-ma is putting together a pie. She makes the best pie.

"Candace, why don't you go get my purse?" she says.

"Gee-ma, I don't need any money. Seriously."

"Don't be silly, just get me my purse."

I walk into the dining room and pick her purse up off the sideboard, trying to ignore the family photos hanging on the wall. My parents' wedding picture, which Gee-ma refuses to take down although I'm sure it makes my dad want to puke. Pictures of Aunt Joanne and Uncle Gary and their perfect lives: on a ski vacation, at the beach, in a Venetian gondola. School pictures of their three kids, my cousins Frank, Allie and Corey. A timeline of well-adjusted young people, smiling smugly down at me from the wall as if to say, *Look at us! Perfectly normal!*

Then there are the pictures of me. A fat, jolly baby, giggling on a pillow at a Sears photo studio. A happy little girl in kindergarten. A cheerful eleven-year-old in a miniature cap and gown, standing onstage at my middle-school graduation. A snapshot of me and Vanessa in party dresses, on our way to our first dance. The pictures stop after my ninth-grade portrait. That one's the worst— no wonder Mom never forced me to have another one taken. I look severely pissed off, and I'm glaring sideways into the distance. I'd given myself a haircut, a poorly done chelsea, and straggly lime-green curls hang down on either side of my face. Even *I* was happy when that cut grew out. God knows why Gee-ma keeps that photo on the wall. Someday it will probably show up on one of those online slideshows of horrible family portraits and I'll go viral for, like, ten seconds.

Poor Gee-ma. I'm sure she looks at those pictures of that cute little kid and compares them to the person I am now. The thought depresses me.

I take her purse back to the kitchen and wait while she rummages around, eventually coming up with a crumpled five-dollar bill.

"Why don't you take this to Bizzby's and buy yourself a milkshake."

"Thanks, Gee-ma," I say, leaning down to kiss her and thinking but not saying that Bizzby's, the tacky fake-fifties diner, is just about the last place on earth I'm likely to end up. I'll save the cash for my next trip to the hardware store.

She grabs my arm as I pull away, and I look down into her face; her usually cheerful smile is gone, replaced with something sad.

"Your father is very depressed these days, Candace," she whispers, although I know he can't hear us over the canned laughter on the TV. "I don't know what to say to him."

I might be kind of a bitch, but come on—as if my heart doesn't melt for my poor grandmother, stuck in a house with my dad.

"I know, Gee-ma," I tell her. "He'll be all right—he's just going through a rough patch." This is the same thing my mother used to tell me when he was going through one of his periods of watching TV for hours in the basement at night. I can't think of what else to say though.

Gee-ma relaxes, and the smile comes back to her face.

"You're such a sweet girl to come here for the weekend and spend time with us. It's good for your father."

I smile, trying not to think about the blaring television and the man in the next room who hasn't said more than ten words to me since I showed up.

"You know," she says, "you're always welcome to visit, anytime you want. You should bring your friend next time. What's her name, Vanessa?"

I nod. "Yeah. Vanessa."

"You two used to come stay with me all the time when you were little girls."

"I don't really hang out with Vanessa anymore," I say.

"Well, that's too bad," she says. "You two were such good friends."

"It's okay, Gee-ma," I say. I lean in and give her another kiss on the cheek. "You have a good night. Save some of that pie for me."

"Of course, dear," she says. "This is for supper tomorrow. I'm going to roast a chicken. You'll be here, won't you?"

Her voice is so desperate that it breaks my heart.

"Wouldn't miss it," I tell her.

"If you make any friends, feel free to invite them along," she says. "The more the merrier."

I just smile. That might be expecting a bit too much.

I should get one thing straight. I did not want to come here for the weekend. It's not my fault that my father is depressed and my mom decided to leave him. It's definitely not my fault that he lost his job and his apartment and ended up living with Gee-ma out in the suburbs.

But even though my dad's issues are not officially my problem, I figured the least I could do was come spend a few days with him. After the worst year of my life, what's one more shitty weekend?

Besides, it's prom night at my school, and I can't think of a better reason to get the hell out of the city. Maybe if I still had friends, I'd feel differently. Vanessa would have spent weeks dragging me along with her to every second-hand and vintage store in the city, finding us something to wear. I'd have probably complained, but I know she would have made us look pretty awesome. If things with Rick hadn't ended the way they did, I might have even had a date. Actually, scratch that—there's no way in hell Rick would ever be caught dead at a high-school dance.

In the porch, I quickly unzip my backpack to be sure I have everything I need. Then I close it up, toss it over my shoulder and head out the door, stopping to glance up and down the street. Gee-ma's house is on one of those streets that reminds you of a hall of mirrors, just one brick bungalow after another. Jesus, the suburbs are depressing.

I think about what Gee-ma said about making friends. Having to spend a weekend here might not be so horrible if I actually knew someone, but meeting people is the last thing on my agenda. If I've learned one thing over the past year, it's that people are better off on their own. Especially when you've got a hobby like mine.

On the sidewalk, I stop and consider which direction to go. It doesn't really matter. I'm on a mission into uncharted territory. It's just a matter of walking until I find what I'm looking for.

I decide to turn left, but after only a few steps I hear laughter, and a gaggle of high-school kids turns the corner a couple of blocks away. Judging from the way they're dressed—blazers and ties, colorful dresses—it's prom night here too. I quickly cross the street and hustle in the opposite direction from the Teenage Zombies From Suburban Hell.

It's going to be a long and painful weekend, I can tell you that much.

ROEMI

Worst. Prom. Ever.

Okay, so you are not going to *believe* any of this. I had a date. To the prom. A prom date. And this boy is hot to trot, fire and brimstone, one sexy little Abercrombie & Fitch-style love interest deluxe.

John. Hot John. I met him online, and he's totally sweet and really cool, and he obviously has good taste in men. We hit it off immediately. I was all *sup* and he was all *nahmuch, you?* and before you know it, we're texting, like, all the time! And not dirty stuff (okay, not *just* dirty stuff—ahem), but mostly just shit like *whatcha doin?* and *just watchin the Kardashians and eatin' cereal.* Shit like that. Cute, right?

All right, so there might have been a couple of minor roadblocks on destiny highway. For one thing, he lives in the city, about a twenty-minute drive away. He's also hard-core closeted, but that's cool, because I was closeted for a while too. Like till I was twelve. The thing with John, though, was that he was going to use my prom as his testing ground for coming out. He was worried for a while that if he came to the Granite Ridge prom, he'd end up seeing someone he knew or someone who knew someone or whatever. Closet stress, perfectly natural.

Anyway, it took a few weeks, but I totally managed to calm him down and convince him not to be paranoid. At least, I *thought* I'd convinced him not to be paranoid.

So the plan was, I'd get dressed up like America's Next Top Male Model, and John would take the bus out from the city and come to my house to pick me up, and we'd go to the pre-prom party at Terry Polish's house and do lots of mingling, and maybe sneak a couple of drinks, and then we'd go to the prom, and there'd be lots of pictures, and he'd meet all my friends, and then there'd be a bunch of fast dancing, and then I'd slip the DJ ten bucks and a jump drive with "Don't Stop Believing" on it, and John and I would end up stealing the show as the lights dimmed and the crowd parted, and then we'd totally fall in love in the middle of the dance floor, melting into each other's arms as the disco ball threw crystal spheres of light down on us.

Best prom daydream ever, right? Totally! We'd be making history!

That's probably worth explaining. See, John and I were going to be the first gay couple to ever own the dance floor at a Granite Ridge High School prom. And yeah, the operative word here is *were*.

So I'm all tuxed up and looking totally fierce, and I've got everything prepared. The lighting is arranged perfectly, my dad is ready with the camera, and I've been training my mother for a week to press Play on my iPod at the exact moment the doorbell rings. I have a really upbeat dance track queued up. At 5:25, we all take our places. I grab the boutonniere I bought this afternoon and perch nonchalantly on the stool that I've placed by the front door. Mom and Dad hang out close by in the living room.

At 5:30, I plaster a million-dollar smile on my face. By 5:40 the smile is a little droopy but still totally ready to snap back to action. By 5:45 I've dropped the smile, but my facial muscles are ready to kick in at any moment. By 5:50 my mouth is starting to twitch in an uncomfortable "we don't know what we're supposed to do, Roemi" kind of way. Also, my backup has decided to abandon me. My dad has gone into the kitchen to make a sandwich, and my mom is on the couch reading a book.

At six o'clock it's official. He's half an hour late, and he hasn't responded to any of my texts. He's not coming. I hop down from the stool and toss the boutonniere onto the entryway table before running upstairs to my room. I slam the door behind me, sit at my desk and open Facebook. Sure enough, there's a DM from John: *I'm so sorry.*

I'm so sorry?! The bastard doesn't even have the decency to text me face to face? Instead I get a three-word Dear John from John on Facebook? Pa. Thetic.

I throw myself on the bed, but I'm too furious to cry real tears, so I resort to stage weeping. I'm loud enough that my parents come upstairs. They stand in the doorway, looking sad.

"Roemi, cheer up," says my dad. "Why don't you come downstairs and we'll have a quick bowl of ice cream, and then I'll drive you to the prom." My dad's solution to everything is ice cream; he rarely had it growing up in India, even though it was the hottest place on earth, or so they've been telling me since I was a kid.

"Listen," I say, sitting up and releasing the death grip on my oldest stuffed animal, Britney Bear, "I'm not going to prom. Prom is ruined. I bragged to everyone about how I was going to make the most spectacular entrance ever. I can't just show up solo and hop out of the backseat of your Land Cruiser like some kind of loser. Can you guys just leave me alone for a little while? I want to lie here and feel sorry for myself."

My mom comes over and kisses me on the head. "I'm sorry, Roemi. Next year, I'm sure you will have the best of all the dates."

"Let me know if you meet him," I say.

"When you feel better, come down and have some ice cream!" calls my dad as they head down the stairs.

I go back to my desk and stare for a while at my computer screen. I feel like I should respond to his message, but even though I usually have no problem being scathing, I'm just too depressed to come up with anything. The thing is, I really like John—or as much of him as I know from the Internet and my cell phone—and I thought he liked me. I put my computer to sleep.

Even though I'm not going to prom, I'm not ready to take the tux off just yet. I get up and stand in front of the mirror. I look awesome. It seems a shame for such a glam-tastic outfit to stay locked up in my room all night. Maybe I don't want to sit around feeling sorry for myself. I quietly walk downstairs. I can hear my parents laughing at a stupid sitcom in the family room. I grab my shades from the kitchen counter and head out the back door.

ANDREA

When I'm out of sight of the house, I text Bethanne.

Bolted—mom driving me crazy

She hits me back right away.

No way! Come 2 Terry's!

Terry Polish's parents let him invite our whole class to his house for a pre-prom party. He lives close to the school, and everyone is planning on meeting there, hanging out for a couple of hours and then walking to the dance together.

I'm not so sure that's where I want to end up. The whole plan for tonight is to make an impression on Justin, and wearing shorts and a *Lake Snelgrove: Come Meet Snelly the Sasquatch!* T-shirt to the prom party is probably the wrong way to do it. On the other hand, the idea of straight up disobeying my mother gives me kind of a rush.

I'll look like an idiot.

U won't—come on!

I consider my options. Really, what else am I going to do? Catch a movie by myself?

ok.

When I arrive at Terry's house, the backyard is full of people, and everyone looks like they're on the red carpet at the Oscars. Unfortunately, I look like I'm on my way to summer camp. Bethanne spots me right away and makes a beeline across the yard.

"Oh my god," she squeals. "You made it! I honestly can't believe your mom is such a bitch!"

"I don't want to talk about it," I say. "You look great, by the way."

"Thanks!" she says. She leans in and drops her voice to a whisper. "So did Lannie and Paul break up or something?"

"I have no idea. Why?"

"She showed up with Ryan and Darrah, but no Paul," she says. "I thought you might know since you and he are friends or whatever."

"We're neighbors," I tell her for the millionth time. "I haven't hung out with him for years."

I look across the yard and sure enough, Lannie is standing under a cherry tree with Darrah and Ryan Penner, but Paul is nowhere in sight.

Paul and I grew up across the street from each other. When we were little, we were best friends. After junior high, when I funneled into academic classes and school band and Paul stuck with sports, we just sort of stopped hanging out. Until the end of tenth grade, we still walked to school together a lot of days. That summer he and Lannie started going out, and now she picks him up every morning. I honestly can't remember the last time I even talked to the guy.

Everyone was pretty surprised when Lannie and Paul started going out. She's basically queen of the school, and Paul is the kind of guy who fades into the woodwork. Maybe that's what appeals to Lannie. That and the fact that he put on about six inches and twenty pounds of muscle during the last half of tenth grade.

I notice a table set up on the patio, with some sandwiches and bowls of chips laid out.

"I'm starving," I tell Bethanne. "I'm going to grab something to eat. Don't go anywhere."

I'm filling a plate when Penner comes stumbling up and pours himself some soda.

"Interesting choice of outfit," he says. I can smell the liquor on his breath.

I glance down at my T-shirt. "Yeah, whatever, thanks."

He pulls a flask from his pocket and pours something into his drink. "You want some?" he asks, shoving the flask toward me.

"No, thanks," I say.

"I should have guessed," he says. "You're probably opposed to drinking or whatever."

"I don't care what you do," I tell him, which is true. "What is it anyway?"

"Tequila and rum and Irish cream liqueur," he says, tossing back a big swig. "Stole it from my old man."

"Oh my god, that's disgusting."

"Does the trick," he says. He takes another big gulp and belches. "'Scuse me."

"Right," I say. "Sure. Have fun, Ryan," I tell him. His mouth is full of chips, so he just holds his cup up and grunts at me.

I take my plate back to where Bethanne is standing.

"What did Penner want?" she asks.

"Nothing," I say. "He's already wasted and it's not even seven. What a loser."

"What do you expect?" she says. "He's got a reputation to keep up." She looks past me and her eyes widen. "Okay, perfect," she says. "Justin is totally standing over there by himself."

I glance over my shoulder, trying not to make it obvious. Sure enough, Justin is standing by the corner of the house. He's staring at his phone, and from the way he's holding it, and the expression on his face, I'm pretty sure he's playing a game.

I know that playing video games at a party like this isn't the epitome of cool, but there's something about it that I find kind of adorable. I wonder why, out of all the guys in school, I have a thing for this one. Justin's hair is always kind of messy, his glasses permanently sit halfway down his nose, and right now his khakis are just an inch or so too long and dragging under his heels, but still… There's just something about his face that gets to me. His lips are full and usually open just enough that you can see the tips of his two front teeth. His cheeks are always slightly flushed, as if he's kind of embarrassed about something. And his eyes, those eyes…pale blue and crystal clear. He's a little bit shy and doesn't say a lot in class, but when he does, when he's talking about something he's interested in, his eyes practically glow, even from behind his bangs.

"Andrea," says Bethanne. "You're staring. Go now. Go talk to him."

"Bethanne, I can't," I say. "I look like an idiot."

"Andrea, please," she says. "He's wearing a tie with a picture of the starship *Enterprise* on it. He's in no position to judge. Now will you go make something happen?" She reaches out and grabs my paper plate, then gives me a push.

Justin is engrossed in his phone and doesn't look up as I approach. I begin to wonder if this was such a good idea.

"Hey, Justin," I say.

"Oh, hey!" he says, looking up from his phone and shooting me a big smile. I start to relax.

"Hey," I say again.

He opens his mouth and is about to say something when Bethanne runs up and practically tackles me from behind. She grabs me by the shoulders and pushes me around the corner of the house. Justin gives me a confused little wave goodbye. I wave back at him.

"What are you doing?" I ask Bethanne.

"Your mom is here," she says.

"What?"

"I just saw her through the window. She's in the kitchen, talking to Terry's mom. They'll be out here any second."

My mouth drops open. "Oh. My. God."

Then I hear her, calling out into the backyard.

"Andrea!"

She sounds 50 percent angry, 50 percent frantic and 100 percent mind-numbingly embarrassing.

"Shit," I say. "What do I do?"

"Just hit the road," says Bethanne. "You're going to catch hell anyway. This is embarrassing enough without your mom dragging you out of the party in handcuffs."

I hesitate, and Bethanne snaps her fingers right in front of my face.

"Andrea! In five seconds you will either be the victim of the most embarrassing moment of your life or the hero of the most badass moment of your life. Now move it!"

She's right. I hurry through the front yard to the sidewalk. Then I start to run.

Sticking to the back streets, I move away from Terry's house and the school. Finally, several blocks later, I slow down to catch my breath. I try to think of someplace to go, somewhere my mother won't come looking for me.

Then I turn a corner and find myself face to face with her. She's wearing her best business suit and her hair is perfectly coiffed. I stop in my tracks and stare at the big fake smile that beams out at me from the side of the bus shelter.

Dinah Wants You to Get Home Now! says the life-size poster of my mother. *Let Dinah Feingold of Feingold Realty Help You Find Your Dream Home!*

"Really?" I ask out loud. Then I hustle past the bus stop, leaving my mother behind to boss around the commuters of Granite Ridge.

PAUL

I'm about to jump into Dad's truck when someone yells at me from across the street.

"Paul!"

I step back from the truck and slam the door. Andrea's mom is waving at me from in front of their house. I wave back before I realize she isn't smiling. She's not really waving, either. It's more like she's beckoning me to come over.

I cross the street. She looks impatient. I've never really liked Andrea's mom; she's strict and not very friendly.

"Hi, Mrs. Feingold," I say.

"Are you going to the prom?" she asks.

"Uh, no. I'm feeling kind of—"

She cuts me off. "Is someone having a party before-hand?" she asks. "Do you know where it is?" She sounds irritated, as if I've done something wrong.

"Uh, I think Terry Polish is having people over to his house." I wonder immediately if I should have kept my mouth shut, since this probably has something to do with Andrea jumping out her window.

"Okay," she says, turning away abruptly and getting into her car. She backs quickly out of the driveway and zooms away toward Terry's house. Now I've probably gone and gotten Andrea in trouble. *Nice one, Paul.*

I get in the truck and drive toward the main strip. I plug my iPod into the stereo jack and scroll through to a playlist I only ever listen to by myself. For one thing, Lannie only listens to divas like Beyoncé and Adele. For another thing, Penner looked through my iPod one day, and he's made fun of me ever since for listening to trip-hop and techno and dance music. He called me a Eurofag, which I guess is his idea of a joke. Whatever. Beats the hell out of the poser fake punk he listens to. M83 blasts at me through the speakers. I jack up the stereo.

I love it when Dad lets me drive his truck. It's a beast, and it totally kicks the shit out of Mom's Corolla. If I could have any job in the world, I'd be a high-end mechanic. I love working with engines and seeing how everything fits together under the hood to make a vehicle run smooth.

I made the mistake of mentioning that to Lannie one time. She didn't like it at all.

"Paul, you don't have to resort to that kind of thing," she said.

"What kind of thing?"

"You know, blue-collar stuff. You're smarter than that. You could be a teacher or something. You just have to focus and work harder." Lannie wants to be a physiotherapist, and no doubt she'll do it—she's definitely smart enough.

I didn't bother arguing with her. When Lannie gets an idea in her head about how things should work out, there's no point discussing any other options. It kind of pissed me off though. My dad's a carpenter, and he runs his own small contracting business. He's always wiped out when he gets home from work, but he's in great shape for an old guy, and every day when he gets home, he cracks a beer and says, "I sure as hell earned this one today." He loves his job. What's wrong with that? But I just keep my mouth shut when Lannie talks to me about education, because I know she just wants what's best for me.

I turn onto Coronation Boulevard, which is what passes for the main strip in Granite Ridge. A Walmart, a grocery store, a bunch of shops and some chain restaurants. If you want to do anything really fun, you have to go into the city, but most of the time people just end up on the strip unless there's a party at the Ledge or something.

I drive by some short dude in a tuxedo walking by himself along the sidewalk. As I pass, I glance in the rearview mirror. Roemi Kapoor. I don't really know Roemi that well. He's in all academic classes, with Lannie and Andrea and the rest of the brains. Penner has a serious hate on for him. He says it's disgusting that we've reached a point in history where someone can be openly gay in high school. He knows better than to lay a hand on Roemi, but he definitely throws a lot of fag talk around when we pass him in the hallway.

I don't agree with Penner about the gay thing. I don't think it's a big deal, but I would never in a million years say that out loud. To be honest, I kind of admire Roemi. When people talk shit to him, he just walks past with his head in the air as if he hasn't heard a thing. It's pretty crazy that someone can be that confident when they've got that kind of heat on them.

Other than Roemi, the strip is pretty much dead. Everyone is obviously at the prom or one of the pre-parties.

On a whim, I pull up to the arcade and go inside. It's full of junior-high kids. A few of them look at me funny, but I figure what the hell and grab a seat at one of the racing games. I get caught up in it for a while, drop a few bucks.

I find myself wishing that Jerry and Ahmed were here with me. We spent a lot of time at the arcade as kids. Now we're a year away from graduating, and I barely talk to them anymore. I could probably stay here all night, playing, but after a few games I force myself to get up out of the little chair and call it a night.

On my way through the parking lot, I decide to stop at the Snak-Stop and pick up some junk food. I'm pretty sure I can convince my brothers to watch *The Bourne Identity* with me for the millionth time.

I grab a few chocolate bars, then head to the chip aisle. I'm trying to decide between sour-cream-and-onion or BlastaCheese nachos when some girl hurries right up next to me out of nowhere, grabs my hand and squeezes it tightly.

I've never seen her before and I'm about to ask her what the hell she's doing when the bells on the door jingle and I see a cop come into the store.

I glance down at her face and can tell that she's scared.

"Please just help me out here," she whispers.

CANDACE

I wander aimlessly for a while before I find a spot that looks like it might have some potential. A little one-story elementary school at the back of a corner lot where two quiet streets intersect. The parking lot is empty, and the school is obviously deserted for the weekend. Just the kind of place I've been hoping to find.

I cross through the playground to the school and duck behind the building. I'm in the dead space behind the school, where a line of pine trees and a chain-link fence partially shield the area from the street. I stick my face up to the fence. There's a sidewalk on the other side of the trees, and across the street are some houses, far enough away that I'm pretty sure they don't have a clear view of the school. A bit farther down the street is a four-way stop sign and some more houses. There's no traffic in sight.

Confident that the coast is clear, I turn and examine the wall in front of me. A big metal box hums quietly at one end of the building, and two large windows sit just above eye level. I get on my tiptoes and peer through one of them into a classroom. I can just make out little desks and little chairs and colorful kids' drawings all over the walls. Between the two windows is an eight-foot stretch of clean brick. It's perfect, the kind of blank slate I'd never find back in the city.

I stop and listen. Other than the electrical box, some kids screaming in the distance and the faraway buzz of a lawn mower, it's dead quiet. In one sense, this is great. It means that nobody is around. On the other hand, it makes me a bit nervous that there isn't at least some traffic to help create a bit of white noise. Spray paint can be pretty loud.

I drop my pack to the ground and unzip it, then bend over and start pulling out my supplies. Five spray cans— brown, two blues, black and red. I know enough to leave them in the pack, upright and sticking out for when I need them, in case it needs to be rezipped in a hurry if I have to make tracks.

The first time I did graffiti—I mean *really* did it, with spray paint, not just markers—I was scared shitless. I'd been out with Rick a bunch of times when he was bombing, but I'd always just stood back and watched. A couple of times we'd had to run for it when somebody got nosy, but he was always totally cool about it.

We'd usually end up in some park, hiding in the trees, laughing our asses off and passing a bottle back and forth. The first time I did it myself, though, it was like I had crossed a line. I was doing something I shouldn't have been, and it felt really good. The thing I liked the most, though, was the final product. We weren't just out smashing shit up or doing drugs or whatever—we were breaking the rules by creating something new.

I uncap a paint stick. When I'm throwing up a new piece, I like to start with a quick outline. Some people use Magic Markers or charcoal; really good artists just slap up an outline with the spray can, but I like paint sticks. They're kind of expensive but worth it—they're slick, so they slide nicely over the walls, and they leave a good crisp edge. They smell really good too.

The trees cast some shadow on me, but it's still broad daylight, so I have to be extra careful. I've been working on this image of a rose. I know it sounds girly, but it's not, really—it's got hard edges and, most important, it's original. I start off with a black outline, then fill in the stem and a couple of thorns with brown paint. I finish the rose with blue—kind of a chalky bluebird-blue for the background, and a deeper blue for the highlights. The final touch is a drop of blood hanging from one of the thorns. I can usually get the whole thing done in about ten or fifteen minutes if I'm working smoothly with no interruptions.

I start sketching, and soon I'm lost in the rhythm of it. Some people are into music, some people play sports, but I get a thrill from the flow of my arm and the smell of the paint.

I finish the outline and reach down to grab a brown spray can. There's a certain skill to filling in narrow spaces—there's no room for error, so you need to make sure you have the distance right. Too close to the surface and the paint will puddle and drip; too far and you'll overdo it, and the paint will feather outside your edges. Either way it will look like shit. I take aim at the ground and shoot a few test blasts, then bite my lip and hit the wall. That's when I hear a car slow down right behind me, on the other side of the fence, and the *whoop* sound of a siren, warning me that I've been spotted.

I'm careful not to turn around, so my face stays hidden. I quickly and carefully bend down and grab my pack, and then I run. I have a good head start, because the cop car has to take two corners to get to the open edge of the schoolyard entrance. Without taking time to think, I dart to the opposite corner of the playground, tossing my backpack into a small playhouse as I move.

By the time the cruiser makes it around the corner and pulls to a quick stop by the entrance of the playground, I've managed to duck behind a garbage can three driveways past the school. I catch my breath and stick my head out just far enough to see a cop jump from the car and run onto the playground. I know it will only take him a minute to realize that I'm not there, so I have to hustle.

As soon as I move out from behind the garbage can, I'll be exposed, so the question is which way to run. Do I take a chance on crossing the street, hoping there will be a clear path to safety? Or do I run up the driveway of this house and into the backyard instead?

I choose the house, because it will save me a few seconds. As the cop hurries back to the cruiser, I stand up and take off for the yard, as fast as I can. I hear him yell for me to stop, and the car takes off with another *whoop whoop*, but I don't look back. I just run.

It's a lucky break that this backyard backs onto another with no fence between them, just some hedges. I race through the two yards and make it to the sidewalk on the other side. Right away, I see the back of a little strip mall across the street. Moving quickly, I make it into the alley between two buildings. I pull off my hoodie and hat as I run, wedging them behind a Dumpster. Then I hurry around the corner and through the first door I see.

It's a convenience store, glaringly bright and pretty much empty. The woman behind the counter is reading a magazine and eating pizza—she doesn't bother to look up at me. The only other person in the store is some young guy standing by a row of chips.

I glance back into the parking lot and catch a glimpse of the cruiser as it pulls in. *Shit.* I smooth my hair down, take a deep breath and walk over to the chip aisle.

The last thing I need is for the cop to recognize me, so without really thinking it through, I reach over and grab the guy by the hand just as the door jingles and the cop walks in. The guy looks at me, startled. Obviously, right? I mean, a strange girl just grabbed his hand out of nowhere.

I look up at him. "Please just help me out here," I whisper.

The police officer stands in the doorway, scanning the store. He stops and talks briefly to the clerk. I can't make out what he's saying, but the clerk just shakes her head and goes back to her magazine. Then he walks over to where we're standing and stops. I try to act as if I don't notice him and reach out to grab a bag of cheese popcorn. Not too surprisingly, the cop won't mind his own business.

"What are you kids up to tonight?"

The dude I've grabbed glances at me, and I can see the wheels spinning in his head. Please don't give me away, I think, hoping beyond hope that he plays along. Then I feel his hand give mine a little squeeze.

"Not much," he says to the cop. "Just buying some chips. We're probably going to just lay low tonight and watch a movie." He turns to me. "So what do you think?" he asks. "Doritos?"

It goes against everything I believe in, but I can't afford to get caught, so I force myself to speak in a sickening baby-doll voice. Anything to avoid sounding like a girl who paints graffiti. "My favorite!" I say. "You know that."

To top it off, I giggle and give him a little bump with my hip.

We both try to ignore the cop, but he just stands there, looking at us. "So you guys aren't heading to the prom?"

"Nope," I say, remembering to stick with the girly voice. "I'm in, like, a huge fight with my friend Tiffany, and I can't be in the same room with her, so we, like, decided to skip it, but she's totally going anyway, probably just to spite me. I mean, I don't understand why some people have to be such bitches, right?"

The cop's eyes start to glaze over. "Yeah, sure, whatever," he says. "Listen, did you guys happen to see a girl running past the store a few minutes ago?"

"What did she look like?" asks my fake boyfriend.

"She had a dark hoodie on and some kind of knitted hat," the cop says. He looks me up and down. "She was pretty much exactly your size."

"Wow," I say. "A five-foot-five teenage girl. Can't be too many of those around." He gives me a dirty look, so I giggle again and roll my eyes for good measure.

"Yeah, anyway, you kids stay out of trouble." He looks like he wants to say something else, but instead he does a slow circuit around the store before finally leaving. As the door jingles behind him, I let out a deep breath.

Fake boyfriend looks at me with a curious, slightly amused expression. I can tell from the way that he's dressed—ballcap and a Nike T-shirt—that he's a bit of a jock, which means that he and I probably have nothing in common. He's cute, though, even if he's not my type. He has short, dirty-blond hair and brown eyes. One of his front teeth twists slightly in front of the other one, which makes his otherwise conventionally handsome face kind of interesting.

I smile at him. "Thanks a million."

"Hey, no problem. Ummm…" He glances down, and I realize I still have his hand in a death grip. I drop it and laugh.

"Sorry. I guess I was a bit stressed-out."

"No worries. So should I call my lawyer? Am I an accessory to murder or anything like that?"

"I promise you it isn't that serious." We both stand there for a moment, smiling. I feel incredibly stupid. "Well, thanks again for your help," I tell him. "Enjoy your chips."

At the front of the store, I stop and look out the window. The cop is still sitting in his car, sipping on coffee. *Shit.* I turn around before he notices me and pretend to stare intently at a rack of magazines.

After a minute, fake boyfriend walks to the counter and pays for his chips. He gets to the door and stops when he sees the cruiser.

"Hey," he says, loud enough for me to realize that he's talking to me. "You coming?"

I pause. The last thing I want is to be around people, but I know that if I walk out of the store by myself, the cop will definitely start hassling me, and I can't afford another run-in. Not tonight.

"Yeah," I say.

He hands me the chips, and I follow him past the cop and through the parking lot to a big pickup truck with a cab on it.

We get in and he starts the engine.

"Where now?" he asks me.

"I guess we could start by getting my clothes back," I say.

ROEMI

For a month, all I've been able to think about is putting on my thoughtfully arranged ensemble and being the center of attention, but after I leave the house and walk several blocks in patent leather shoes, I wonder if I should have changed into jeans and Adidas. It's difficult to be inconspicuous when you're wearing a tuxedo with purple-satin accents. Even on prom night. After several cars honk, and someone throws a balled-up fast-food bag at me, I begin to wish I'd just stayed home.

You might find this surprising, but downtown Granite Ridge isn't the most inspiring place in the world. Even so, as I trudge along the sidewalk I do my best to feel like a heartbroken hero in a melodramatic Italian movie. Unfortunately, you can only hear the latest Bieber single blasting out of car windows so many times before the foreign-film fantasy bursts.

I walk all the way to Bizzby's, the 1950s-style diner that opened on the strip a year ago. Even though it's part of a chain, Bizzby's is definitely my favorite place in town. With its pastel colors and curvy windows, it's the closest thing to a Hollywood movie set that you're going to find around here. It has a big neon sign across the front, and they keep the place clean and shiny. They even make the servers wear diner uniforms and name tags with fake fifties names on them, like Peg and Chet.

I grab a seat at the counter, on one of the cushion-topped chrome stools, and do a couple of obligatory spins. A scowling twentysomething hipster wearing an apron and a little paper hat walks over and holds out a menu. I wave it off and glance at his name tag.

"No need, Biff. I already know what I want. Gimme an extra-large double-fudge Hurricane shake, and hey, what the hell, toss in a couple extra squirts of chocolate sauce."

It's probably a bad idea. Milkshakes almost always make me want to puke, but I know I have to man up and throw caution to the wind. My dad wouldn't hesitate to tuck into that milkshake. He'd probably down it in one go and then slam the glass down on the counter and tell Biff to pour him another one.

While I wait for my drink, I put my head in my hands and try to figure out what exactly went wrong with John.

I've been telling him for weeks how great the prom is going to be, and I thought he was as excited as me. None of this makes sense, and after the big deal I made about the whole thing, I feel like a total chump.

Biff puts my milkshake down on the counter and I settle up, then head back out into the night.

I don't feel like going home yet. I find myself wandering down back streets, lost in my thoughts. Sure, lately John had started mentioning that he was kind of scared of going to the prom, but I thought I'd done an awesome job of selling it as a sort of baby step on the journey of coming out. He was clear from the start that nobody else knew he was gay, but everyone has to come out sometime, right?

I turn a corner and I'm suddenly face to face with my old elementary school. It looks so tiny now, compared to when I was small. I walk onto the playground and sit in a swing to finish my milkshake. When we were kids, the world was well defined and easy to wrap your head around. The rules of the playground were straightforward. You knew who the bullies were, you knew where the teachers on duty stood, you knew which girls were willing to play *American Idol* every day at recess. None of this confused love-connection crap.

A shiver runs down my spine. At first I think it might be an ice-cream headache starting, but I can't shake the feeling that I'm being watched. I turn around slowly and realize that there are two small faces peering at me from inside the small playhouse on the other side of the sandbox.

"Who's in there?" I yell, beginning to feel like I'm in a twisted horror movie.

After a moment, two little kids crawl out of the playhouse and stand at a distance, looking at me suspiciously. There's a girl of about ten and a little boy a couple of years younger than her.

"Why are you dressed like that?" the girl asks—a bit rudely, if you ask me. I find kids creepy at the best of times, but I especially dislike the ones who aren't polite to adults. I know I might only be seventeen and I'm easily the shortest guy in my class, but as far as I'm concerned, I should qualify as a grown-up to a ten-year-old.

"Dressed like what?"

"In a suit," she says, pointing. "With all that purple stuff."

"I'm the tooth fairy," I tell her. "This is my uniform. Are you kids allowed to be over here by yourselves?"

The girl, who is obviously in charge, takes a step forward. "We live right over there." She points toward some houses across the street. "We come here all the time."

"Well, why don't you guys scram?" I've always wanted to tell someone to scram.

She sizes me up for a second. I can't believe I'm having a standoff with a fifth-grader. Finally she shrugs and turns to her brother. "Okay, Frankie, let's go." Then she says in a very loud, very distinct voice, "Don't forget your *backpack*."

She turns and raises her eyebrows at him. He looks confused for a second, then ducks back into the playhouse. When he emerges, he's dragging a bulky black backpack.

As they march past me, the girl turns briefly and looks at my cup. "Milkshakes'll rot your teeth, *tooth fairy*." I sneer back at her and watch as they hustle through the playground and stop to look both ways before darting across the street to their house. Little Frankie hobbles along behind his bossy sister, bent under the weight of his oversized backpack.

No sooner have the kids disappeared behind their house than a truck pulls up by the sidewalk. A girl jumps out and comes running onto the playground toward the play area. What's next, a military marching band? So much for alone time.

She looks like she's in a big hurry, and she doesn't notice me until she's almost at the swing set. She stops in her tracks and quickly looks me up and down. I take a slurp of my milkshake.

"Hey," she says. She's around my age, but she definitely doesn't go to my school. She has a small silver nose stud, and her hair is very cool. Jet black, with a thick blue streak in her bangs.

"Hey. You planning on mugging me or something?" I ask.

"Um, no," she mutters as she kneels down by the playhouse door. "Shit!" she yells.

"Looking for a backpack by any chance?" I ask. She spins around to face me.

"Do you have it?" she asks. "Hand it over—it's mine!" She sounds frantic.

"Take it easy," I tell her. "I don't have it, but I'll tell you where it is if you calm down. If you'd been here thirty seconds earlier, you would have caught them yourself."

"Caught who?"

I point across the street. "A couple of kids. They were hiding in there when I showed up, and then they scurried home, dragging your pack behind them. You just missed 'em. Come to think of it, it seemed strange for a little kid to have the anarchy symbol sewed onto his backpack."

"Shit!" she says again. "My wallet's in that pack, and all my—other stuff."

I finish my milkshake with a noisy slurp and hop down from the swing. "You want some help getting it back?" I ask her, tossing my cup in the nearest trashcan.

She doesn't sound too enthusiastic. "I think I can manage," she says.

"Suit yourself, but I do know what the kids look like, and I'm bored out of my skull."

She pauses and looks at me as if considering my offer.

"Okay, why not?" she says. "If you're sure you don't mind."

"Trust me," I say. "This is the most exciting thing that's happened to me all night. I'm Roemi, by the way."

"Candace," she says. "You coming?"

I follow her as she runs back to the truck. My shoes make it a struggle to keep up.

It's safe to say that Paul York is the last person I'm expecting to see. From the look on his face, the feeling is mutual. I don't exactly have a problem with Paul, but you can tell a lot about a person by the company he keeps, and Ryan Penner is some douchey company. I swear, someday I'm going to break out my slickest moves and kick that bastard's ass.

"My pack's missing," says Candace. "Roemi here said he can help me find it. You guys know each other?"

"Yeah," we say at the same time.

"What's up, Roemi?" he asks.

"What's up yourself? Shouldn't you be at prom?" I ask him. "Where's Lannie?"

"Long story," he says. He obviously doesn't want to talk about it, so I bite my tongue. Always difficult.

"I don't want to break up your little reunion," says Candace, "but can we get a hustle on? I don't want to be here when the cops show up again."

"Excuse me?" I say. "Cops?"

She doesn't answer me, so I look at Paul. He shrugs. "She won't tell me," he says.

"Okay, hang on," I say. "I'm not helping you with anything unless you fill us in. What's the big secret? Is there a head in that backpack?"

"No," she says, exasperated. "Nothing like that. It's nothing, it's just—it's nothing. It doesn't matter."

We both stare at her. She lets out a long groan. "Okay, fine," she says. "You'll think it's stupid, but whatever. I need that pack because it has all my graffiti stuff in it."

"Graffiti?" I repeat. "Really?"

"Yes," she says. "I was bombing the back of that school and some cop showed up and almost caught me. I threw my pack into the playhouse and ran to the nearest store. That's when I met Paul, and he told me he'd help out. I told you you'd think it's stupid, but I don't give a shit what you think."

"Relax, Rembrandt," I tell her. "Nobody said anything was stupid. Do you think it's stupid, Paul?"

"No," he says. "I'm actually kind of relieved. I thought you were dealing or something."

"As if," says Candace.

"Is it really such a big deal to the cops?" I ask. "Graffiti, I mean."

"Yeah," she says. "You can get in real trouble. Vandalism charges. Trespassing. Break and enter, if you're in the wrong place at the wrong time."

I point across the street. "I'm pretty sure that's the house the kids went behind."

We backtrack through a couple of yards and duck behind a hedge at the back of their lot. Sure enough, the kids are in the backyard, about twenty feet away from us.

They're playing some sort of game that seems to consist of the girl bossing Frankie around. The backpack is nowhere in sight. "That's them," I whisper.

"Are you sure?" asks Candace.

I nod just as the kids stop what they're doing and turn abruptly toward the house. A screen door swings out, held open by the arm of an invisible adult. The girl seems to be having an argument with whoever is standing inside.

"I'll do it later!" she yells. She stops and listens to something, then throws her hands up in frustration and follows the arm inside. Frankie stays outside.

"Okay," says Candace. "I'll be back in a minute." She starts to move, but I grab her arm.

"Listen," I say. "Don't be offended, but if you jump out of the bushes at this kid, he's going to think that he's being abducted by the angel of death. He'll be in therapy for years, if he doesn't die of shock first. Let me do it."

I run into the yard and over to Frankie.

His jaw drops when he sees me. "Tooth fairy?" he asks, his eyes wide.

This is something I can work with. "Yes!" I say. "It's me, the tooth fairy! Where's your sister?"

"Mom made her call Grandma for her birthday," says Frankie. "I already talked to her today, so I'm allowed to stay outside."

"Well, boy oh boy, Frankie," I say. "Have I got a surprise for you!"

"A surprise? But I haven't lost any teeth lately."

"Umm, that doesn't matter! Because you—have won—the tooth fairy lottery!"

"Whaddaya mean?"

"All you have to do is answer one skill-testing question, and you get the grand prize! Just tell me where the backpack is and you'll be the winner!"

"You mean the backpack from the park? The one with all the hairspray in it?"

"Yeah, that one!"

"My sister hid it behind the toolshed."

"Excellent! Good job! You're the winner!"

"What do I win?"

"Ummm…" I reach into my jacket and pull out my wallet. No cash, just cards. "Hang on a second." I run back to the hedge. "Quick!" I say. "Do either of you have any cash?"

"I told you, my wallet's in the backpack," says Candace.

"What's the deal?" asks Paul. "Is he holding it ransom?"

"I don't have time to explain. Come on, I need some cash!"

Paul digs into his pocket and shoves a five-dollar bill at me. I run back to Frankie.

"Who were you talking to?" he asks.

"My reindeer," I say. "He carries my wallet."

"You have a reindeer? Lemme see!"

"He's invisible. Listen, kid, I've gotta get moving. These lottery prizes won't deliver themselves." I shove the fiver at him.

"Wow!" says Frankie. "Five bucks! Thanks, tooth fairy!"

"Yeah yeah, no problem." I quickly glance at the house. "Where's the backpack?"

He trots behind the toolshed and comes back a moment later with the pack.

"Thanks, buddy," I say, turning to make my getaway. "Remember to brush and floss, and don't play violent video games!"

Back at the hedge, I hand the pack to Candace. "You've got one hell of a heavy hobby," I tell her. "Let's get out of here."

Once we're in the truck, she rips open the pack and rifles through it, pulling out cans of spray paint and plastic bags full of markers.

"Awesome," she says. "Everything's still here. I don't know why I even bothered to take this shit with me. It's not like there's anyplace worth painting in this bullshit town."

"I wouldn't be so quick to judge if I were you," I tell her.

ANDREA

Granite Ridge got its name from the abandoned quarry that's half hidden in the woods on the east side of town. Because one side of the quarry is a steep wall of granite that rises above the tree line, everyone calls it the Ledge.

When I was a kid, my mom made it very clear that I was to stay away from the quarry. She said it was a place where bad people went to do bad things. When I was eight or nine, I saw *Dirty Dancing* on TV, and for a while I was convinced that the Ledge was a hangout for people like Patrick Swayze and his dance crew. I pictured girls with giant blond hairdos and tight leather pants hanging off guys with slicked-back hair and denim jackets with the sleeves cut off. In my imagination they built bonfires and passed around bottles of whiskey before choreographing elaborate dance routines under the moon.

When I got a bit older, I overheard my brother talking to one of his friends about a party at the Ledge, and it occurred to me that if it really was a place where bad things happened, Brad was one of the people responsible. By the time I reached high school, it was clear that the Ledge was just a place where pretty much every teenager in my high school went to party.

Except for me. I've never been to a Ledge party, and I know I'm one of the very few people in my grade who hasn't. Even Bethanne goes sometimes. She's tried to convince me to tag along, but I'm just not interested. The occasional house party is okay, but hanging out in the woods with a bunch of drunk people isn't my idea of a good time. I'd rather stay home and read.

Although I've never been there, the trail is easy enough to find. I'm amazed at how much garbage people have dropped along the path. Every couple of feet, a beer can or fast-food wrapper has been dropped on the ground or thrown into the bushes. I haven't gone very far before the trees thin and I walk into what must be the quarry. It isn't very big or impressive, just a gravelly area that's been cut into the side of a hill. Some beat-up old chairs and a couple of milk crates have been dragged into a circle around a charred hole in the ground. The hole is full of even more garbage, which is blackened and melted.

I walk around and check the place out. The bottom of the wall is covered with lame graffiti, stuff like *Karl loves*

Marla and *GRHS Grads of '95*. I obviously haven't been missing much by staying away.

I don't know what I'm doing here, but I take a seat on a milk crate anyway.

Maybe if I was the kind of girl who thought it was fun to party at the Ledge, who was able to smuggle booze into her room without getting caught, who hasn't always listened to her mother, I wouldn't have to chase Justin. Maybe he'd be the one chasing me.

Then again, I *did* jump out of my bedroom window. I *did* make a mad escape from Terry Polish's house. Besides, it's stupid to think that the best way to get a guy to like you is to act like an idiot.

My cell phone rings and I pull it out. Mom, for the millionth time. I turn off the ringer and shove it back into my pocket.

What's the use? I'm not going to change anything by staying out all night. I'm just making my mother angrier the longer I stay away. I'm about to walk home and face the music when I hear voices.

I don't know what I'm expecting. Maybe some college kids home for summer break and looking for a trip down memory lane. I can tell you what I'm *not* expecting: Paul York, some sullen girl I've never seen before and Roemi Kapoor in a full tuxedo with purple-satin accents. In the complicated social scene at Granite Ridge High, Roemi Kapoor and Paul York are not what you'd call best friends.

"Andrea?" says Roemi as they push through the bushes and into the clearing. "Why aren't you at prom?"

"Looks like I should be asking *you* the same question." I point at his outfit.

"Yeah, no kidding." He rolls his eyes. "It's a tragic story. I don't really wanna talk about it. This is Candace, by the way," he says, pointing at the new girl. "She's me and Paul's new best friend."

I look at Paul. He shrugs slightly and gives me an embarrassed smile.

"Hey," I say, holding out a hand to the new girl. "I'm Andrea."

She has a backpack hanging over her shoulder by one strap. She stares at my hand and then shifts the weight of her pack to reach out and shake. She seems annoyed by the effort.

"What are you guys doing here anyway?" I ask.

"It's kind of complicated," says Roemi. "Candace here is a hard-boiled criminal, and she almost got caught in the act by the cops, but she made a daring escape and then took me and Paul hostage, and now she's forcing us to participate in her evil schemes. Speaking of which," he says, turning to Candace, "this is the place I was telling you about! Ta da!"

I have no idea what they're talking about. Candace must notice the confused look on my face. "I was bombing," she explains. "Doing graffiti. Or trying to, I guess. Anyway, these guys said this might be a good spot."

Graffiti? Seriously?

She drops her backpack on the ground and walks over to look at the Ledge.

"For real though," says Roemi. "Why aren't you at prom?"

"Well, I guess the main reason is my mom's a bitch," I say. I tell them about the hidden booze and getting grounded. About jumping out the window and the scene at Terry's house. I obviously don't mention Justin.

"It's kind of my fault that your mom showed up at Terry's house," says Paul. "She cornered me in my driveway. Sorry, Andrea. I wouldn't have said anything if I'd known what was going on."

"Don't worry about it," I say. "I know better than anyone how pushy she can be. Why are you here anyway? Did you and Lannie break up or something?"

Paul shakes his head. "Nah, nothing like that."

"Don't even bother trying to get any info out of this guy," says Roemi. "Paul's being very mysterious this evening."

"Well, what about you?" I ask. "You're obviously all dressed up with nowhere to go."

Roemi closes his eyes and sighs deeply. "If you must know, I was stood up."

"Oh that's right," I say. "You had some big date planned, didn't you? First gay prom couple at Granite Ridge?" He's been talking about it for a month.

"Yeah, *had* is the right word. As in, I've been had. The bastard left me crying at the altar."

"Did he have an excuse?" I ask.

"Nope, just a one-line message on Facebook saying he was sorry. He's sorry, all right—he's a sorry son of a bitch. Anyway, what can you do?"

Candace walks over to us. "This isn't going to work," she says, pointing at the rock face. "There aren't any good spots left." We look at the wall. She has a point. Every square inch is covered with crappy paintings and Sharpie autographs.

"It's no big deal," says Candace. "It was worth a shot."

"Okay, wait," says Roemi. "We're already missing out on prom; we can't have a massive fail with this too. There must be someplace for you to get all artistic and shit. What are you looking for? What would be the perfect place to do this?"

"Something smooth and flat," she says. "Something that doesn't have a bunch of other shit already painted on it." She cranes her neck and points up the side of the wall. "Like up there."

"It's, like, fifteen feet high," says Roemi.

"That's a total heaven," she says.

"What do you mean?" asks Roemi.

"A heaven is a hard-to-reach place," she says. "Hard to get to and hard to remove once it's been painted on."

"Kind of dangerous, don't you think?" I ask.

"Exactly," she says. "As in, you could die and go to heaven."

"If it's so dangerous, then what's the point, exactly?" I ask.

She shoots me a dirty look. "The point?"

"The point of risking your life to get to someplace dangerous just to paint graffiti," I say. "I guess I don't understand why anyone would want to do that. It's only going to end up upsetting people anyway, isn't it?"

She looks at me with such contempt that I instantly feel as if I've just said the stupidest thing ever.

"I really don't give a shit if it upsets someone," she says. "And I definitely don't give a shit that you don't understand."

Roemi lets out a long, low whistle. I shrug and try to look like I'm not bothered by her rudeness. It's not like I'm trying to offend her. I really don't understand why anyone would want to climb up a cliff to spray-paint something that's just going to annoy people. Plus it's illegal.

"Would it help if you had an extension ladder?" asks Paul. "There's one in the back of my dad's truck."

"Are you kidding me?" asks Candace. "Can I use it?"

"No problem," he says.

The thought of being an accessory to a crime isn't very appealing to me, especially since I'm already in big trouble with my mother.

"I think I'm going to get out of here," I say.

"Oh, come on, Andrea," says Roemi. "Live a little. What else are you going to do? Exams are over, remember? There's nothing left to study."

"I don't know," I say. "I don't really want to be involved in, you know..."

"Breaking the law?" asks Candace, half laughing, half sneering. "Let her go," she says. "She's scared. Big deal."

"Come on, Andrea," says Paul. "It'll be fun. Something different."

"I'm not scared," I say.

Suddenly the last thing I want to do is give this strange girl the satisfaction of thinking I'm leaving because of her. I don't really understand what Paul thinks will be so fun, but I have as much right to be here as anyone. Besides, it's not like I'm going to be holding the spray can. To hell with her.

"I guess I've got nothing better to do," I tell them. "I might as well stick around for a while."

"Oh goody," says Roemi. "We're all best friends again."

"Whatever," says Candace, without so much as glancing at me. She looks at Paul. "So let's go get this ladder."

PAUL

Candace and I walk back out to where I've parked the truck. I pop the door to the cap and lower the tailgate.

"So do you usually do this with other people when you're in the city?" I ask as Candace and I haul the ladder out.

"No," she says, shaking her head. "I used to, but now I keep it to myself. It's easier that way."

"What about your friends?" I ask.

"What about them?"

It's obvious that she doesn't want to talk about it, so I drop the subject.

"I like being by myself," she says eventually. "It's kind of hard to explain, but this is important to me. It's my art, and when people think it's stupid, I'm not going to go out of my way to change their minds."

"I don't think it's stupid," I say. I don't bother to tell her that I definitely would have said it was stupid before I met her.

"Yeah, well, most people do. Your friend back there does."

"Who, Andrea?" I ask. "Nah, Andrea's cool. She's just a really responsible person. I don't think she meant anything by it."

"I know when someone's judging me. I'm used to it, but that doesn't mean I have to like it."

We carry the ladder back to the edge of the woods and lay it down on the side of the path.

"I'm going to grab some rope," I say. "Safety first."

We go back to the truck, and I rummage around until I find a coil of rope. I'm crawling back out of the truck when a car pulls up and parks behind us.

"Shit," Candace whispers. "Five-oh."

It's the same cop from earlier. He gets out of his car and walks over to us.

"Well, will you look at this," he says. "I thought I recognized this truck. You guys aren't up to any trouble here, are you?"

"No, sir," says Candace in her fake baby-doll voice. "We just came to the park for a stroll. It's superduper romantic here!"

"Got to be careful," he says. "You'll find yourself in all kinds of trouble if you start getting too romantic in a public space, if you catch my drift."

"Oh, for sure!" says Candace. "I'm saving myself for my wedding night."

I choke back a laugh. She sounds totally sincere but completely naive, and none of it lines up with the way she looks.

"That hoodie looks familiar," the cop says, pointing at Candace.

"You like it? My grandma bought it for me before she died. It really means a lot to me." She makes a sad face.

"You guys mind if I take a look inside the vehicle?" He's already walking around it, looking through the windows.

"Be our guest," says Candace. "We're not doing anything wrong."

"Yeah, I think I'm going to have to take a little look-see inside the cab." He looks at me. "This your truck?"

"Yeah," I say. "Well, it's my dad's truck."

He gets me to pull out my license, insurance and registration. He looks them over, then cheerfully opens the front door of the truck and starts to dig around.

We stand to the side, and Candace nestles up against me, shoving her face into my chest and biting on her knuckles. I put my arm around her and play along, trying not to imagine what Lannie would think if she saw this whole scene.

After several minutes, in which the cop turns the cab upside down, empties all of my dad's toolboxes and even gets on his back and shines a flashlight underneath the truck, he stands up and reluctantly hands the papers back to me.

"Nothing in there," he says.

"That's what I said!" says Candace, her voice muffled by my shirt.

"Listen," he says, "I think it's about time you guys hit the road. There's no good reason to be hanging out here."

"Yes, sir," I say. "We'll do that."

I wait for him to get back in his car, but he doesn't move. He just stands there with his arms folded, staring at us. "Not sure if you guys understand what I'm saying here," he says. "I think you should leave. Now."

"Okay, wait a minute," says Candace. "You can't just make us leave. We aren't doing anything wrong, and this is a public space!"

"You're right," he says. "I can't legally force you to leave, and I can't charge you with anything if you decide you want to ignore my advice and stick around anyway. But you know, I don't have to go anywhere either." He looks up at the sky and whistles. "It's an awfully nice evening to just sit here and listen to the radio." He looks at his watch. "I'd say the prom isn't going to be over for at least, oh, I'm guessing another few hours or so. Until then, I won't have a whole lot to keep me busy."

He takes a step toward us. "I'll tell you something else. I don't trust either of you as far as I can throw you. I knew there was something fishy going on back at the convenience store, but you convinced me that you weren't the girl I was looking for. Now I'm pretty sure I was right all along. Give me some credit, guys. You think I don't know about the Ledge? I know you kids don't go in there to play board games."

I don't see any point in arguing with him, especially since he's right, but that doesn't stop Candace.

"And people wonder why teenagers hate cops," she says.

"Nah," he says. "Nobody wonders about that. Everyone knows teenagers hate cops because cops are always keeping teenagers from doing dumb shit. It's pretty straightforward. I've been around awhile. I might not be able to prove anything, but I promise you that if you give me any reason at all, I will have no problem making hay with it. I take vandalism very seriously."

"Come on," I say, putting my hand on Candace's shoulder. "Let's go."

"You should probably listen to your boyfriend, sweetheart. You guys go home and make some popcorn and stay out of trouble. By the way, you must really think I'm stupid if you think I'm buying that fake voice you're using."

Candace makes a face at him but follows me to the truck and jumps into the passenger seat. She rolls down the window and sticks her head out. "Oh hey, *officer*," she says in her normal voice. "I've got some advice for you too. Don't call girls *sweetheart*. It's sexist, and it makes you sound like a pervert."

I pull away from the curb.

"Asshole," she mutters.

"What should we do?" I ask as I circle out of the cul-de-sac. "I can't leave my dad's ladder back there—he'll kick my ass."

Candace turns around and looks out the back window. "What the fuck? He's still following us!"

I check the rearview. She's right; the cop is trailing close behind us. I turn onto one street, then another, and he follows me both times. He's definitely sticking to me on purpose.

"Okay," says Candace. "This is starting to feel like creepy hillbilly shit. Doesn't he have anything better to do?"

"I doubt it," I say. "There's not a hell of a lot going on around here tonight. At least, not until prom is over. He's just messing with us because he's bored."

"Stupid cops."

I pull onto the main drag, then into the parking lot at Bizzby's. Sure enough, the cop pulls in and parks a few spots away from us. We look over and he grins and waves at us.

"Oh my god, what a jerk!" says Candace.

"Okay, this is stupid," I say. "We're not going to shake him. I'm going to take the truck home and get my mom's car. Then we'll go back and get Andrea and Roemi. I'll deal with the ladder later."

I pull out of the parking lot and the cop follows, creeping on my bumper all the way to my street. When I get to my house and pull into the driveway, he slows down and watches as we get out of the truck.

Finally he drives away, with a brief honk and a wave. Candace gives him the finger. "*Hasta la vista,* asshole!"

My mom's car isn't in the driveway, and the door to the porch is locked. "I don't know where they are," I say as I unlock the door. I stand to the side and hold the door open for Candace. "Come on in."

CANDACE

You can tell a lot about someone by seeing where they live. Until that point, the only information you have to go on is the way a person dresses and talks, maybe the music they listen to. But being inside someone's house, it's *intimate* or something, like all of a sudden you have a whole new set of clues.

I remember the first time I saw Rick's apartment. He lived with his dad, who worked night shifts, so we would go there a lot. The first time he took me there, I remember noticing how dingy everything was. Not much furniture, dirty dishes in the sink, an overflowing ashtray in the middle of the coffee table. When he opened the fridge to grab us some beers, I noticed that there was almost no food. But it was his room that really caught me by surprise. The walls were covered with a giant graffiti mural in progress—he'd actually spray-painted the walls of their rental apartment. I'd never even heard of a thing like that.

Obviously I knew that graffiti was his thing—that was how I had met him, standing around in the shadows, watching him and his buddies throw up a huge burner underneath an overpass. To see how seriously he took it though—living in the middle of it…It was inspiring to see that kind of dedication.

Paul's house, by contrast, is more of a standard suburban two-and-a-half-kids kind of place. In the porch, hooks are overflowing with coats for all seasons, and shoes and sports equipment jockey for space with full recycling bins. I stand in the doorway and look around as he walks into the kitchen and reads a note stuck to the fridge.

"They've all gone to a movie," he says. "Shitty. Guess we won't be taking my mom's car after all." He opens the fridge. "You want something to eat?"

"No, I'm good."

He pulls a bowl of potato salad out of the fridge, grabs a fork and starts eating. "I'm starving. Just give me a minute."

"Sure."

"Hey, come on in, you don't have to hang out in the doorway like that," he says, his mouth full of food. "Sure you don't want a Coke or something?"

"Yeah, why not?"

He points at the fridge. "Grab me one too, will ya?"

I get the drinks and then stand for a minute, looking at the pictures that are plastered all over the fridge door. A few random pictures of babies and some wedding photos. Paul with people who must be his parents. Paul with two younger boys who look almost exactly alike. They're posing on bikes, having a water fight, sitting for school photos.

"Twins?" I ask.

"Yeah, my brothers. They're thirteen."

"Oh my god," I say, pointing to a picture of a short scrawny teenager in a suit, standing next to an old man. They're both grinning broadly. "Is this you?"

He laughs. "Yeah, me and my granddad at my aunt's wedding. A couple of years ago."

"Holy shit," I say. "You must have gone through one hell of a growth spurt after that." I stop at a more recent picture of Paul with a tall healthy-looking girl with a confident smile and long strawberry-blond hair. Paul is standing beside her, smiling awkwardly.

"This your girlfriend?" I ask.

"Yeah," he says, reaching past me to open the door and put the potato salad back in the fridge. "That's Lannie."

"She's hot," I say.

"Yeah, well, that's Lannie. Listen, I'm gonna run to the bathroom. Make yourself at home."

While I wait, I walk into the living room and look around. On one long wall, next to more family pictures, is a shelf full of trophies and ribbons, most of them with Paul's name on them. I was right: total jock.

Paul comes bounding back down the stairs, two at a time.

"So," he says. "What do you think we should do?"

"I don't know," I say. "Your friends must be wondering what happened to us."

"Yeah, no doubt. They're probably long gone by now."

"Yeah."

Then there's silence. It fills the room, and we both just stand there, looking at each other with no idea what to say.

"Well," I say, turning toward the kitchen and breaking the moment, "I should leave. I've got to go get my backpack."

"Why don't I come with you?" he says. "I have to figure out what to do about that ladder anyway. It's not that far to the quarry, if you know the right shortcuts. Besides, it's only nine o'clock. I'm not ready for bed yet."

I shrug. My plan of lurking around town by myself has already gone to shit. Besides, I don't mind spending time with Paul. He isn't someone I can imagine being friends with in my real life. He's *the perfect teenager*, all clean-cut and rosy-cheeked. The kind of guy who scores the winning goal in the important soccer game, says his prayers before supper and is always nice to his parents. He's the exact opposite of Rick, in other words, but there's something about him that makes him easy to be around.

He's right about the shortcuts. He leads me through backyards and across parking lots and before I know it, we're back at the Ledge. Sure enough, Roemi and Andrea are nowhere to be seen.

"Shit!" I say, realizing that my backpack isn't where I left it. I look around frantically, but it's gone.

"Those guys must have taken it," said Paul.

"I sure hope so. My wallet's in there, my keys—everything." I sit on a rock. "This is turning out to be kind of a bullshit night."

"Yeah, I guess so," he says.

"No offense."

"Well," he says, "there's no way I can carry that ladder home, even if you help me. I'll have to try and sneak out of the house and drive back to get it before my dad gets up for work tomorrow."

I nod, depressed about my backpack.

"So why don't we go see if we can find those guys?" he says. "They must be looking for us if they took your pack."

"Yeah, you're probably right."

Paul leads the way out of the woods, and we wander along quiet suburban sidewalks. It's so different from being in the city, where every block has people on it, and every building is lit up.

"So where are we going?" I ask.

"Not really sure," he says. "I figure we'll walk to the strip and see if they're wandering around or something."

The strip, no surprise, isn't much busier than the back streets. A few cars drive past us, pulling out of fast-food drive-throughs, blasting shitty top-40 music. The more we walk, the more preoccupied Paul becomes. He's just drifting along as if he doesn't remember I'm with him.

"Can I ask you something?" I say. He looks at me and nods.

"Why did you help me back there? At the convenience store, I mean."

He thinks about it for a second. "I guess I could tell that you really needed help, and you looked like the kind of person who doesn't ask for it very much from people. All I had to do was pretend to look at chips with you. And hold your hand. Not too tough."

I nod and we continue walking. "Why aren't you at the prom with your girlfriend?" I blurt out.

He stops in his tracks and turns to me. We're standing at the bottom of a little grass embankment that rises up to a Walmart parking lot. It's kind of gross. A patch of matted dead grass, cigarette butts all over the ground. A crushed beer can sits next to a garbage bin.

Paul doesn't say anything for a second. Then he bursts out laughing and drops to the ground. He lies down on his back and stretches out, surrounded by little bits of garbage and bald patches in the grass. I sit down next to him and try not to think about how many dogs have pissed in this spot.

"I don't know," he says. "I don't know, I don't know." He sits up and looks at me. "Okay, I do know." He starts laughing again. I wonder if he's having a nervous breakdown.

"I do know," he says again. He takes a deep breath. "It's not like you know anyone around here, so what the hell. I have panic attacks. Do you know what a panic attack is?"

I nod.

"Well, I have them sometimes. I used to have them all the time, when I was a kid." He pauses, chewing on his lip. "I usually had them the night before a test or during report-card week. Anything that was kind of stressful could set me off. My parents wanted to send me to a summer camp when I was about eleven, and I had such a bad attack in the car on the way there that they stopped and turned around."

He lies down again and puts his hands over his face. He laughs quietly but not happily. I check to see if there's anything gross behind me, then lie down beside him.

"So anyway," he says. "I had these attacks for a few years, and so my parents sent me to a psychologist, and by the time I was in junior high, they were happening less and less frequently, and then they just kind of stopped. Which was great because they tended to get in the way of…I don't know, everything. But then, this year, like literally over the past couple of weeks, they started up again." He sits up. "I mean, what the fuck?"

"What do you think brought it on?" I ask, standing up and brushing myself off.

"Who the hell knows?" he asks. I reach down and give him a hand up. There's a candy wrapper on his shoulder. I reach up to flick it off. We start walking again.

"This morning I woke up to the sound of a text from Lannie," he says. "It's no big deal, she texts me all the time, but today…I guess it was the prom that set me off, maybe the pressure of it. It's stupid, I know, but…"

"You had another attack," I say.

He nods. "Yep. Luckily, my mom was around, and she's been through it with me before, so she knew what to do. She called Lannie and made up an excuse for me, so I didn't have to deal with it myself."

"How'd that go over?" I ask.

"Like a ton of bricks," he says, smiling. "I'm just happy that I didn't have to talk to her."

"You don't sound too worried about it."

"Well, Lannie's a bit of a control freak, but she'll come around. It's not the end of the world. I'm sure I'll be making up for it all summer though."

His face falls a bit.

"What did your mom tell her?" I ask him.

"Oh, that's the best part. She said I had diarrhea, that I must have eaten some bad clams or something. Who knows how she came up with that."

He starts laughing. He has one of those laughs that is totally contagious, and before I know it we're both doubled over, tears streaming down our cheeks.

After a while we manage to calm down, and Paul wipes his eyes. "You know," he says, "I think that's the first time I've seen you laugh all night."

"I was just thinking the same thing about you," I say.

We're standing there, and the traffic is whizzing by in both directions, and it's that moment when the sun has gone down past the buildings but it still isn't down over the horizon, so the air is totally clear and everything is vivid and colorful. Even the signs on the fast-food restaurants and the Walmart and the Canadian Tire across the street are kind of beautiful. I grin at him because it strikes me that this is so different than what I expected when I left Gee-ma's house a few hours ago.

"What is it?" he asks, smiling back at me.

"Nothing," I say, shaking my head. "It's just funny. All of this."

"Yeah," he says. "It's turning into kind of a weird night."

"Do you want to maybe go somewhere and get a coffee?" I ask him.

"Yeah," he says. "That's exactly what I want to do right now."

ROEMI

Oh, Andrea. Poor hermetically sealed, under-socialized, fashion tragedy Andrea. I've always thought the term *nerd* was outdated. You might as well call someone a *hepcat* or a *wench*. However, when the shoe fits, wear it. In this case, the shoe is a denim flat with a ribbon on it, which more or less proves my point.

When Candace and Paul leave us to get the ladder, Andrea immediately starts asking me what I thought about our exams.

"Andrea, please," I say, after listening to her drone on about chemistry class. "Exams are over for the year. Do you really want to do a play-by-play recap? Can't you save some of this for one of your online science-group chats or something? You're going to bore me to death."

"Well, what do you want to talk about?" she asks.

"Let's talk about how this is the worst night of my life. Let's talk about how I should be at the prom right now, bumping and grinding with the love of my life. Let's talk about my very personal human tragedy."

"Yeah. That's pretty crappy," she says. She doesn't sound nearly as sympathetic as the situation warrants.

"Yeah," I say. "Crappy like the end of the world, I guess."

"Oh, come on," she says. "It's prom, not your wedding. You have your whole life to meet guys."

"Yes, and I intend to meet lots of them," I say. "But in the meantime, I'm supposed to be having the best night of my life. Instead I'm with you, in a wrinkly tuxedo, waiting for Paul York to sneak his dad's ladder into the woods so we can help some weird goth girl paint the Ledge. Forgive me if I'm a little heartbroken."

"What do you think is taking them so long?" she asks, ignoring a second great opportunity to console me.

"Who knows? Maybe they decided to drive to the hardware store and pick up some scaffolding."

"No, seriously," she says. "They've been gone for a while. Let's go see if they need help or something."

When we're almost out of the woods, we come across a ladder lying beside the trail.

"Weird," we both say at the same time. Sure enough, the truck is gone too.

"What do you think?" I ask. "Is your money on a practical joke, a torrid affair or an alien abduction?"

"I doubt she would have left her pack behind without a good reason," says Andrea. "Something must have happened. Maybe somebody showed up and they had to leave."

She has a point. "What do you think? Should we wait for them?" I ask.

Her response is typically lame. "I think I should probably start walking home," she says. "I might as well face the fire sometime."

"Oh my *god*, Andrea," I say. "You ran away from home! You're going to get punished anyway, right? So you might as well take advantage of the situation in the meantime. Otherwise it's like stealing a Ferrari, taking it out to run errands and maybe do some volunteer work and then returning it."

"Well, what do you suggest?" she snaps. "Should I wander around behind you all night, listening to you whine about being stood up?"

"Oh snap," I say. "That was kind of harsh."

"Yeah, it was, wasn't it?" She looks embarrassed. "Sorry about that."

"Don't worry about it." I shrug. To be honest, it's the first real sign of life I've seen from her all night.

"Seriously though," she says. "What should we do?"

"Let's get out of here and see if we can find them," I say. "It'll be like an adventure."

"Not much of an adventure," she says.

"Work with me here," I tell her. "Who knows? Maybe they got arrested and we'll have to break them out of jail!"

"Well, if we're going to leave," she says, "we should do something about Candace's backpack."

"What do you care?" I say. "She was kind of a bitch to you."

"I don't want her stuff to get stolen though," she says. "Maybe we should take it with us."

"It's pretty heavy," I tell her. "Besides, we don't even know where they are. If we leave it here, at least she knows where she last had it."

"Yeah, that makes sense," she says. "But we should hide it, in case someone else comes along."

"You're very moral," I tell her. "If someone talked to me the way Candace talked to you, I'd probably put dog shit in her bag instead of putting it away for safekeeping."

We go back into the quarry and Andrea shoves the pack deep into a thick shrub. Then we start walking toward the strip.

"You know," I say, "I actually think I have a legitimate reason to be upset. I was really looking forward to tonight."

"I know," she says. "I'm sorry I was such a bitch. Sometimes I think I take things too seriously."

"No shit," I say. "Weren't you looking forward to prom?"

"I was," she says. "Believe it or not."

"Getting dressed up and dancing all night is pretty much the best thing ever," I say. "I bet Justin would have thought you looked hella hot."

"What are you talking about?" she asks, turning quickly to glare at me.

"Ouch! Enough with the devil eyes," I say. "Come on, Andrea, it's common knowledge that you have the hots for Justin Sanchez."

"Well, *I* sure never said that," she says, as a slow blush rises up into her hairline.

"Oh, Andrea," I say. "You have so much to learn. Okay, let me put this in terms you can understand. It's like you're the sodium to Justin's chloride. For example, I sit right behind you in chemistry class, and I've noticed that every time Justin raises his hand to speak, your whole body shifts."

"I pay attention whenever anyone in class speaks," she says.

"Sure, but when other people speak, you just sit there with the end of your pencil in your mouth, looking at the ceiling. When Justin opens his mouth, you turn to look at him and your eyes get all wide and dreamy like some girl in a Japanese cartoon. Trust me on this one. I could draw your swoony, slack-jawed love profile from memory."

"Whatever."

"Hey, don't be offended," I say. "There's nothing wrong with digging on a guy. Justin's cute, in a strange, geeky, scientist hipster sort of way. You guys would make a good couple."

"I'm not offended," she says. "I'm embarrassed. Is it really that obvious?"

"No, not at all. The only way I picked up on it is that I have excellent straightdar. I'm sure nobody else notices."

"Really?"

"Not really. You practically drool when he walks into the room."

"Oh my god." She starts chewing her nails.

"Relax," I say, grabbing her hand and pulling it away from her face. "I'm just messing with you. And quit that right now. Nail-biting is gross and unhygienic."

We turn onto the strip. We haven't even walked a block when a minivan full of jerks drives by and some yahoo tosses an empty soda bottle at me. It misses me narrowly.

"Hey, faggot!" the guy yells.

Andrea jumps back, startled. I reach down and pick up the bottle and whip it at the van.

"Tell your dad he left his undies at my house, asshole!" I yell.

Andrea turns to stare at me.

"Asshole!" I yell again as the van disappears into the distance.

She won't stop staring. "What?" I ask.

"Jesus, Roemi," she says. "Those guys. They just…did they just…?"

"Yes, Andrea, they screamed a homophobic slur at me."

"Do you know them?"

"I don't know—they drove by too quick. They might have just been yelling because of my outfit. I do kind of look like the master of ceremonies in *Cabaret*."

"Are you okay?" she asks.

"I'm fine," I tell her. "I don't really want to talk about it."

"Okay," she says. She's still looking at me though.

"Andrea," I say, "it's fine. It's Granite Ridge—it's a hazard of the landscape. I can't wait to get out of this place. Aren't you excited to graduate and get the hell out of here?"

"I don't know," she says. "I guess I don't really think about it that much."

"Well, I think about it," I say. "I think about it every fucking day. Anyway, where do you suppose Paul and Candace are? This adventure is starting to suck."

"Your guess is as good as mine," she says, looking up and down the street.

"Well, let's just walk this way," I say. "Maybe they'll drive by us or something." I pull my phone out of my pocket. Nothing from John.

"What are you looking at?" asks Andrea.

"Just seeing if Monsieur Dickhead had a change of heart."

"And?"

"Nada. He's obviously making out with a football player or something as we speak."

"Oh, come on," she says. "He must have had a good reason for standing you up. Didn't you get any hints from him or anything?"

"We weren't playing twenty questions, Andrea," I say. "Besides, it's hard to pick up on that stuff online."

"Are you telling me that you never met this guy in person?" she asks.

"Of course not," I say. "We video-chatted all the time though. That counts, right?"

"I don't think so," she says. "I don't get it. I thought you were, like, the king of dating or something."

"You obviously weren't listening. I told you I had great straightdar. I'm great at helping girls figure out boys and giving fashion tips and stuff. In case you haven't noticed, I'm the only out gay student at Granite Ridge High School. I haven't had much personal practice with dating."

"So you don't know anything about this guy except for what you learned online?"

"Hey, don't knock Google! I know what his parents do, I know where he lives, I even found supercute pictures of him playing Little League a few years back. We're practically engaged."

"Yeah, but Roemi—"

"Hey," I say, putting my hand up to cut her off. "Can we stop talking about this? I know the whole thing was stupid and I should never have expected it to work out. I just don't really want to admit any of that right now. I want to feel hard done by. I want to wallow in self-pity. If I wanted to answer questions about my failed date, I'd be at the prom right now talking to my real friends about it."

"Okay, I get it," she says. She starts walking briskly ahead of me.

I feel like a total asshole. She's just trying to help.

"Hey, wait up!" I say, hurrying after her although I think my shoes are starting to kill the nerve endings in my feet.

"On a more cheerful note, I'll bet you that with my help we could make Justin fall head over heels for you."

She stops and waits for me to catch up, turning around and raising a skeptical eyebrow at me.

"Seriously," I say. "Justin is the kind of guy who needs to be told what's going on. He's a bit spacey, if you know what I mean. He's not going to figure this thing out on his own, but with some prompting, I guarantee you guys could be married by graduation."

She laughs. "That's what Bethanne tells me. She says that if I like him, I'm probably going to have to make the first move. She says he has no skills."

"Well, Bethanne's a wise woman," I say. "Despite her bangs."

"That was kind of the main reason I wanted to go to prom," she tells me. "I was going to talk to him, or whatever."

"That's as good a plan as any," I say. "Talking is usually a good first step."

Andrea's attention drifts past me. "Check it out," she says, pointing across the street.

I turn and see Paul and Candace sitting inside the Starbucks. We cross the street to the coffee shop and stop outside, watching them through the window. They're a mismatched couple, to say the least, but it actually kind of looks like they're on a first date or something.

"Man oh man," I say. "If Lannie saw this, they'd both have to go into the witness protection program."

I knock on the window and Paul waves, beckoning us in. The look on Candace's face is harder to read. I wonder if she wants us there at all.

"What happened to you guys?" I ask, taking a seat.

Paul and Candace go back and forth as they tell us the cop story. "My dad's going to kick my ass if I don't get his ladder home tonight," Paul says, leaning back into his seat.

"Can't you just go home and get the truck again?" asks Andrea.

"That cop was being a total asshole," says Candace. "If we go back up there in the truck, he'll be all over us."

"What about my parents' Land Cruiser?" I ask. "It has a roof rack. Would the ladder fit on top of it?"

"Are you serious?" says Paul. "That would totally work. You don't think your parents would mind?"

"They'd be thrilled to help," I tell him. "They're very enthusiastic people."

"That would be awesome, man. Thanks!" he says.

I glance past him as a couple of women come in and walk up to the counter. "Uh, Paul," I say. "I know you don't want to talk about it, but does Lannie have any idea that you're spending prom night hanging out with the Breakfast Club?"

"What? No, so please don't mention it next time you see her."

"That's not what I'm getting at," I say. "Don't turn around now, but her mom just walked in."

"Shit!" he says, slouching down in his seat.

"Okay, listen," I say. "The important thing is not to panic." I turn to the girls. "I'm going to make a distraction and then you guys hustle Paul out of here. Try to keep him covered."

"Roemi, he's a foot taller than either of us," says Andrea.

"Just do your best, and wait for the right moment." I jump out of my chair and run over to the counter, where Mrs. Freston and her friend are waiting for their coffees. I quickly move around in front of her to keep her facing away from our table. "Hi, Mrs. Freston!" I say.

She actually jumps a little bit, startled. "Oh, Roemi. You scared me. How are you?"

"I'm fine, Mrs. Freston," I say cheerfully. I make a quick motion with my hand, signaling for Paul and the girls to leave. Paul shakes his head and points past me at the door. I know what he means—if they run for the door, Mrs. Freston will definitely see him. But she'll also see him if she turns away from the counter with her drink. We're stuck between a rock and a hard place.

I just stand there, smiling like an idiot. My mind races, trying to figure out what to do. I'm obviously interrupting them, but I can't lose their attention.

"Do you like my tuxedo?" I ask.

"It's very...colorful," she says. "Why aren't you at prom?"

"Oh, it's a long story, Mrs. Freston," I say. "I guess you could say I'm president of the lonely hearts club this evening.

Drowning my sorrows in a skim macchiato with an extra shot of espresso, a pump of vanilla and whipped cream. I know the whipped cream kind of defeats the purpose of the skim, but you know what they say, yin and yang. The circle of life and all that."

Behind her, Paul and the girls move slowly through the coffee shop and stop just out of Mrs. Freston's line of sight. The barista reaches over and places two drinks on the counter next to the ladies, who appear happy for the excuse to turn away from me.

"Well, it was nice to see you, Roemi," says Mrs. Freston as she moves to grab her drink.

"Wait!" I say. They turn back to me. Mrs. Freston's friend looks a bit nervous. Hard to blame her—it's not every day a short gay teenager in a purple tuxedo screams at you in a Starbucks.

"Wait just one second," I say. "I promise you'll be happy you did. Has Lannie told you about my amazing new act?"

"No, I don't believe she has." The look on her face tells me that Mrs. Freston is running out of patience.

"I'm surprised she hasn't. All the kids at school are super impressed with it. I'm hoping it gets me a scholarship or something. Okay, cover your eyes. You too, ma'am," I say to her bewildered friend.

"What? Roemi, this is all very strange."

"Please!" I say. "It will just take a second, and I'm having such a horrible night, I'd love to bring some joy into someone else's evening."

"Oh for heaven's sake, Diane," says her friend. "Let's just watch his act."

"Thank you, ma'am! Now cover your eyes, and no peeking!"

Reluctantly, Mrs. Freston puts her drink back on the counter, and she and her friend cover their eyes. I motion for Paul and the girls to hustle. As they scurry out of the coffee shop, I say, "Okay, ladies, on the count of three. One! Two! Three!"

They drop their hands, and I break into a snappy little tap dance. I improvise by twirling in a circle and even throw some jazz hands into the mix before stopping with a flourish, flipping an imaginary top hat down my arm. Mrs. Freston doesn't look very impressed, but her friend claps politely.

"That was pretty good," says the barista from behind the counter.

"Thanks! I'm here all week," I say as I turn and race to the door. "Goodbye, Mrs. Freston," I call over my shoulder. "Say hi to Lannie for me!"

The guys are waiting around the corner of the building.

"Did you seriously just tap-dance for Lannie Freston's mom?" asks Andrea.

"It was either that or my Michael Bublé impression," I say. "Now let's get out of here before they decide to leave." I point dramatically toward my street. "To the Roemicave!"

ANDREA

Roemi's house is the kind of place my mom would kill to have on her listings sheet. Most houses in Granite Ridge are pretty boring, mainly bungalows and split-levels. Roemi's, however, is a contemporary castle, all glass and steel and exposed wooden beams, sitting on a perfectly landscaped hill. He leads the way up the front walk and shoves the huge front door open.

"I'm home!" he hollers.

Sticking together and staying a few feet back, the rest of us follow him into the house. The place is enormous, with soaring beamed ceilings and expensive leather furniture. In front of us, a large steel staircase leads to a landing with a bunch of doorways opening off it. It feels like a movie star's house.

Candace stops in front of a giant abstract painting.

"This is incredible, Roemi," she says.

"Yeah, my parents love that artsy shit." He cups his hands over his mouth. "I'm home!" he yells again at the top of his lungs.

"Hello, dear!" The voice comes from somewhere deep inside the house.

"They're in the family room," Roemi explains. "Probably watching reruns of *Friends* or something. They love sitcoms. Come meet them. Don't worry about your shoes. The cleaning woman will be here tomorrow."

As we follow him, Candace turns to us and mouths, "Wow!" Paul and I nod in agreement.

The family room is actually more of a home theater. A gigantic TV takes up most of one wall, and big plush armchairs and couches are lined up in front of it. There's a popcorn machine and bowls full of candy on a table in the corner.

Two smiling people get up from their chairs as we come into the room.

"Hello, dear!" says his mom. "We wondered where you went. Hello, Roemi's friends, I'm Roemi's mother." She looks at Paul and smiles. "You must be Roemi's boyfriend, come to take him to prom after all."

Candace snickers as Paul turns red.

"As if," says Roemi. "This is Paul and Andrea—they go to school with me—and this is Candace. She's a traveling gypsy artist."

"Oh, how wonderful, an artist," says Roemi's dad. "What kind of work do you do? Do you have anything for sale at the moment?"

This time, Candace looks uncomfortable. "Um, no, not really. Thanks for asking though."

Roemi's dad beams at Candace, and his mom beams at his dad, and then they both turn and beam at Roemi. There are some good vibes in this room.

"Roemi," says his dad, "why don't you take your friends to the kitchen and give them some ice cream?"

"No, thanks, Dad, we're in a rush. Can we borrow the Land Cruiser?"

His dad frowns slightly and squints at Roemi. "The Land Cruiser? Who's going to be driving?"

"Paul," says Roemi. Paul's eyes widen, but he doesn't say anything.

Roemi's dad turns to Paul, his cheerful face suddenly stern. "Do you have your driver's license, young man?"

"Uh, yes sir," says Paul. "I've been through driver's ed and got my full license a couple of months ago."

"And there will obviously be no joyriding or going over the speed limit?"

"For sure," says Paul. "I mean, I'll drive safe. No speeding."

"There will be no drinking and driving, will there?"

"Dad!" says Roemi. "No drinking and *anything!* Come on, I promise."

Roemi's dad thinks about it for a moment, his face deadly serious.

"Okay then," he says. "As long as safety comes first. Use your seat belts!" He smiles broadly again. "The keys are hanging on the wall in the garage."

"Great, thanks," says Roemi. "Come on," he says, turning to the rest of us. "Let's go up to my room so I can throw some jeans on."

"Nice to meet you," I say to his parents as Roemi hustles us out of the family room.

"Have fun!" they say in unison.

Roemi's bedroom is as impressive as the rest of the house, although quite a bit messier. Sliding glass doors open onto a little balcony, and a bright white bathroom is visible through a doorway. On one side of the room is a sitting area with a couch and an armchair that faces a desk with a massive computer monitor on it. A goldfish in a bowl sits on top of a mini fridge. Plastered all over the walls are Abercrombie & Fitch ads of muscular shirtless guys; a giant poster of Lady Gaga hangs over the bed.

"Roemi, what the hell?" says Paul as soon as we're in the room. "You didn't tell me I'd be driving."

"Well, I can't do it," says Roemi. "I don't even have my learner's permit. What's the big deal? Anyway, grab a seat," he tells us. "I just have to figure out what to wear. There's soda and stuff in the fridge." He rummages through piles of clothes and quickly comes up with a pair of jeans and a neon-green T-shirt. He goes into the bathroom and closes the door but comes back out again almost right away.

"Can't do it," he says. "I look too good in this tux. I'm paying for it too, so I might as well get my money's worth. I'll just put sneakers on."

I drop into Roemi's incredibly comfortable couch. "I could get used to this, Roemi," I say.

"Tell me about it," says Paul.

It's kind of strange to be hanging out somewhere that isn't either my house or Bethanne's. It's even stranger for the four of us to be here together.

"Your parents seem really cool, Roemi," I say.

"What do they do?" asks Candace.

"Dad's a family doctor and Mom's a shrink," he says.

"Do they want you to be a doctor too?" asks Paul.

"No way," says Roemi. "Only if I want to be, which I don't. Gross. As long as I find something I enjoy doing and work hard at it, they're pretty much cool with whatever."

"Must be nice," I say. "My mom has been pushing me to go into engineering since I was a kid."

"Is that what you're going to do?" asks Paul.

"Probably," I say. "It pays well, and I'm good at math and science."

"Way to live your own life," says Candace, who's sitting with her legs over the edge of the armchair.

"What's that supposed to mean?" I ask.

"Oh, come on," she says. "You know what I mean. Sounds like your mom is part of the system, and you're just lining up like a sheep to do as you're told."

"What system?" I ask her.

"You really don't have any idea, do you?" she says. "Let me guess. Your mom also wants you to go to the university in the city, so you can live at home and save money and she can keep you in her sights. You'll study really hard and get good marks and eventually you'll end up in some boring job that you hate, but you'll do it so you can make money to pay for a house just like the one you live in now. Then you'll have some kids and eventually they'll grow up and you'll push them out into the world to do the same thing."

"Heavy," says Roemi.

"You don't know anything about me," I say, although she's kind of hit the nail right on the head.

"I don't need to know you," she says. "Because I know plenty of people *like* you already. People who hear the word *graffiti* and immediately jump to conclusions, because they've been told what to think their whole lives."

Paul looks really uncomfortable, as if he wants to be somewhere—anywhere—else. Roemi, on the other hand, is leaning forward in his chair as if he's front row center at the best show in town.

"I don't know what you're talking about," I say. "I didn't mean anything about the graffiti thing.

I was just *asking* you why you wanted to do it. I wasn't trying to insult you."

"It's not even that," she says. "It's all the preconceptions. I can see it in your eyes, in the way that you talk about it. It's true, isn't it? You prefer to not think for yourself, so when you meet someone who's willing to break the rules, it makes you uncomfortable. It's not your fault. You've been conditioned that way."

"I think for myself," I say. "I broke out of my house, didn't I?"

"Oh, that's right," she says. "And you've only mentioned going home about ten times in the last hour. Face it. You'd rather take orders from people, like your mom, or the cop who's been harassing me all night."

"You mean the cop who's just doing his job?" I ask her.

"His job?" she says, her jaw dropping. "So it's his job to harass teenagers without good reason?"

"You were breaking the law," I say.

"And why is it the law? What fucking difference does it make if I want to make public art? It's like we're living in a police state or something."

"Public art? Give me a break," I say. "Since when is vandalism art?"

"If you feel so strongly about it," she says, "why don't you just make a citizen's arrest?"

"Ladies," says Roemi. "Puh-leaze. Enough with the catfight. We have an adventure to go on." He stands up. "Let's get out of here."

My head is spinning, and I'm not sure what I did to make Candace hate me so much, but I don't want to stick around to find out.

"Sorry, Roemi," I say. "I think I should probably go home now."

Candace laughs. "Go ahead," she says. "Prove my point for me. The minute someone shakes you out of your comfort zone, you're racing home to Mommy and some well-deserved punishment."

"Don't leave, Andrea," says Paul. "I can give you a ride home later."

I don't even bother responding. I just grab my backpack and walk out of the room, hurry down the stairs and push through the heavy wooden door and out of Roemi's house.

PAUL

I don't know what made Candace go off on Andrea. It's true that Andrea plays by the rules, but it's not like the rest of us are big lawbreakers or anything.

"What was that about?" Roemi asks Candace after Andrea leaves.

"I don't want to fucking talk about it, okay?" she says. "I don't even know where I am. Can you drive me to my grandmother's house?" she asks me. "Please? One-five-five Highview Street."

"If it's okay with Roemi," I tell her.

"Yeah, whatever," he says. "We should go back to the Ledge first though. We need to get the ladder back. Also your backpack."

"Shit!" says Candace. "I forgot all about my pack. It's probably been stolen by now."

"Doubt it," says Roemi. "Andrea took great and deli-cate care in hiding it for you." He tilts his head and stares at her, his eyes wide and innocent.

"What?" she snaps at him.

"Nothing," he says. "Just thought you might like to know."

"Can we just go?" she asks.

"Sure!" he says. He turns to me. "Isn't this fun?"

Roemi's parents' garage is nicer than my parents' living room. It has heated floors and shiny chrome over-head lights. It also has a gleaming new Land Cruiser and a goddamn Audi A4.

I walk slowly around the Audi, standing a few feet back so I don't drool all over it.

"Roemi, this is an Audi A4."

"Oh yeah? Is that good?"

"Uh, yeah," I say. "This is a supernice car."

"Huh. Yeah, my dad loves that car. I don't like the color." He grabs a set of keys from a hook on the wall, double-clicks them to unlock the Land Cruiser and tosses them at me. "I'm obviously shotgun," he says to Candace.

Candace climbs into the backseat. "This is bigger than my bedroom," she says. I stand at the suv, my hand on the door handle, but I'm still staring back at the Audi. Roemi reaches over and opens the door from the inside.

"Come on, Paul! Let's go, dude!" he says.

Reluctantly I get behind the wheel and slide the keys into the ignition. Roemi reaches over and presses the garage-door opener on my sun visor. The door slowly rolls up, and Roemi jacks the volume on the stereo. "Let's roll, bitches," he says.

The Cruiser is totally pimped out. Leather seats, wood veneer, a kickass stereo. But as sweet as this ride is, as we pull out of the garage I wonder if I'll ever have the chance to drive anything half as nice as the Audi.

It doesn't take long for Roemi and me to get the ladder and strap it to the roof rack. Roemi tells Candace where to find her pack, and she runs to the quarry to get it. She comes back just as I'm hooking the last bungee cord.

"I have an idea," says Roemi. "We should cruise by the school and check out the last-minute rush into the dance. We're pretty close. Let's do a drive-by."

I'm not sure I want to risk being seen by Lannie, but I can't very well say no, since it's his car.

Luckily, the crowd at the school is so involved with checking each other out that nobody takes a second glance at the Land Cruiser. I park across the street from the school and we watch through the tinted windows as girls run screaming to greet each other and smokers take their last drags before ditching their butts and walking onto the school property.

"Hey, Paul," says Roemi. "There's the old ball and chain."

Sure enough, there's Lannie, walking across the street in front of us, just a few car lengths away. I slouch down in my seat.

"Relax," says Roemi. "Nobody can see us unless they get up really close to the window. She looks fierce."

She really does look good, with her hair piled on top of her head and her dress hugging her body in all the right places. The funny thing is, I don't have any interest in being out there, walking into the dance with her. I'm happier here, hidden behind the tinted windows.

"Okay," says Roemi, "I still don't really get this. So you and Lannie didn't break up, right?"

"No," I say.

"But you aren't at prom with her, and she doesn't know that you're spending the night hanging with the Scooby-Doo crew?"

"No," I say. "She thinks I'm sick."

"I know you don't want to talk about it," he says, "but I'm going to give this one more shot. Now that we're all besties, can you please just give us the Coles Notes version of *The Case of Lannie Freston's Missing Prom Date*? The curiosity is killing me."

I glance in the rearview and see Candace raise an eyebrow at me. Suddenly it all just seems stupid and pointless.

"Fuck it, whatever," I say. "I had a panic attack, okay? I had a panic attack last week for the first time in years, and then this morning I had another one, and it was so bad that I couldn't even think about going to the prom. So my mom called Lannie for me and told her I was sick, and that's why I'm not at the prom tonight."

"I'm not sure I understand," says Roemi. "Why didn't you tell Lannie? She's your girlfriend, after all. Wouldn't she understand?"

How can I explain that because Lannie is so *in* control, I'm terrified of letting her know I am so *out* of control? That if she finds out what's wrong with me, she'll see it as another challenge? She'll try to fix me, make me better.

Maybe I should let her. She's fixed everything else. My friends, my future, my grades, the way I look, the things I do in my spare time. Why shouldn't I let her fix this?

"Maybe he's not at the prom because he didn't want to go in the first place," Candace says quietly. I look at her in the rearview mirror again, and she shrugs and looks me straight in the eye as if to say, *Isn't it true?*

"Whoa, check it out," says Roemi, pointing past me. I turn to see Ryan Penner walking away from the crowd in the parking lot and up onto the street where we're parked. At first I think he might have spotted us. Then he reaches into his jacket pocket and pulls out what looks like a baggie, and I realize he's just sneaking away to smoke a joint before going inside.

Sure enough, we watch as he lights up and strolls directly toward the Cruiser. He stops with his back to my window and then begins to pace back and forth, furiously working through the joint.

"I don't think he sees us," I say quietly.

"This is like a horror movie," says Roemi. "Don't breathe or the homophobe will get us!"

"Who is that guy?" asks Candace.

"That's Paul's best friend," says Roemi. I shoot him a dirty look.

Penner finishes the joint and crushes it out on the ground. Then he leans down to look in the window of the Cruiser, his face just inches from mine.

"Oh my god," whispers Roemi. "I'm going to shit my pants!"

Penner brushes his fingers through his hair and straightens his tie. I slowly let out my breath. He's just using the window as a mirror. But then he leans in really close, and I watch as recognition rolls across his face. He taps on the window.

Reluctantly, I roll it down.

"What the fuck, man?" he says. His eyes are blood-shot, and he's obviously stoned and drunk. "Lannie told everyone your appendix burst and you're in the hospital."

"False alarm," I tell him.

He pulls a flask from his jacket pocket and hands it through the window to me. He reeks of booze, and he's swaying on his feet. "Want a drink?" he asks.

"Nah, man, I'm cool."

"Suit yourself." He takes a big swig and shoves it back into his jacket. "Who you rolling with anyway?" He bends down and sticks his face into the suv.

"Hi, Penner!" says Roemi. He grins widely and gives a little wave.

"What the fuck?" says Penner, pulling his head back like he's been burned. He looks at me with his mouth hanging open, and then he starts to laugh.

"Are you seriously telling me that you ditched out on Lannie fucking Freston to hang out with this queer?"

"No, man. It's not like that," I say, painfully aware of how weird the whole thing looks.

"I'd rather be gay than stupid and ugly, Penner!" yells Roemi.

The back door of the suv swings open and Candace jumps out. She walks over and pokes Penner in the chest. "Who the hell are you?" she demands.

He staggers back, bewildered. "What the fuck is going on, Paul?" he asks me.

"Nothing man. We were just—"

"I *asked* you a question!" says Candace, getting right up in Penner's face.

"Whoa, whoa," he says, throwing up his hands and stepping back from her. "I'm not going to get into anything with some crazy emo bitch."

"Emo?! Oh my god, who the hell is this guy?" she asks, turning to look at me.

"He's just a friend."

"Some friend," she says.

"Penner, come on, man," I say. "Why don't you walk it off?"

"Man, what the hell is going on with you anyway?" he asks me. "Why are you out here with these losers instead of inside with Lannie fucking Freston? Have you lost your mind?"

"It's not like that," I say again. "I needed to borrow his truck to run an errand."

"An errand?" He shakes his head as if he can't believe what he's hearing. "What-the-fuck-ever, York. This is some crazy shit, man." He turns and staggers back toward the school. I figure it won't be long before Lannie knows everything.

I lean back in my seat and close my eyes.

"Wow," says Candace, still standing outside the vehicle. "Nice work standing up for Roemi, Paul."

"What was I supposed to say?" I ask.

"I don't know. How about 'don't talk shit about my friend Roemi'? Something like that?" she says.

"You don't understand," I say. "I can't just get into it with him. Ryan's a good friend of mine."

"Oh, and I'm not?" says Roemi. "I see how it is. To hell with you." He opens the door and swings his legs out of the Cruiser.

"Jesus, Roemi," I say. "He was drunk. I was trying to keep it from turning into something big."

"Yeah," he says. "I should just let it slide off my back, right? Fags like me should keep our mouths shut and be happy we're not getting beaten up, right?" He jumps out of the car and starts speed-walking down the street.

"Whoa, Roemi," I yell after him. "What about the Land Cruiser?"

He stops in the middle of the road and looks back at me. "Just bring it back to my parents' house and put the keys in the mailbox," he yells before starting to run. He takes the corner and is gone. Candace stands next to the window, shaking her head at me.

"You know," she says, "you almost had me fooled. I should have known you were just a poser."

She reaches into the back of the suv and pulls out her backpack. She slams the door and throws the pack over her shoulder. Then, without glancing back, she takes off down the street after Roemi.

CANDACE

It was my tenth-grade art teacher, Ms. Jonas, who really helped me to see that art is everywhere, that it can be anything. She taught me that buildings, and photos of buildings, and paintings and sculptures that get hung in buildings, can all be seen as art. Even shitty art is art, and you can even take shitty art and look at it in a different way and all of a sudden it's not shitty anymore.

It's all subjective, Ms. Jonas would say, which is a fancy expression that basically means "beauty is in the eye of the beholder."

I loved Ms. Jonas's class. It made me look at things differently. I'd been sketching since I was a little girl, but before Ms. Jonas's class, it was mostly just boring stuff. Drawings of my cat or the view of the street from my window.

Then I opened my eyes and realized that the world was full of amazing art. It was everywhere—not just in art galleries but on the sides of buildings, underneath bridges, on the backs of billboards. Graffiti is the kind of thing you don't really notice until you start looking for it; it just kind of blends into the background. But when you actually begin to seek it out, you realize it's like a secret creative language that only the initiated can understand.

It didn't take long till I was starting to think about doing it myself. I began carrying around a ziplock bag full of Sharpies. At first I was too scared to consider tagging in a public space, so I just practiced a lot by drawing designs on the backs of my notebooks and shit like that.

One day after school it was raining, so I took the bus home. I was bored and staring out the window, and I just kind of found myself drawing some random design on the flat piece of aluminum under the window. It was small, and there was already lots of crap written all over the walls, so I figured it was no big deal.

Then I looked over and saw an old lady across the aisle staring at me. She was shaking her head and giving me a really dirty look, as if I was the scum of the earth. I got embarrassed and stopped, but for the rest of the day, all I could think about was how that lady reacted.

The world is full of people like that old woman. People who think life is about following rules. Like Andrea. Maybe I shouldn't have been so hard on her, but I just get so sick of people who have their entire lives all figured out, one prearranged step after another. If I ever get to that point, you have my permission to shoot me.

It turned out Vanessa was like that too. You think someone's your best friend, and the minute you pull away from the crowd and try to do something different, they throw you under the bus for it.

I thought Paul was different, that he was capable of thinking for himself. The truth is, he was just putting up a front. He just needed a quick break from his perfect girlfriend and his asshole friends, so he spent a few hours pretending he was his own person. But when push came to shove, he showed that he's ready to fall in line too, just like almost everyone else.

At least Roemi has the balls to be the person he wants to be. I try to catch up with him, but when I turn the corner, he's gone. I have no way of knowing which direction he's gone in, so I pull out my phone and map out the best way to walk to Gee-ma's house.

I'm almost halfway there when I come upon some kind of municipal works building. I stop and look at it. It's small and squat and ugly, just a cinderblock building with a pale-gray metal door. A bright streetlamp on a tall pole shines a dull green light on the building.

The street I'm on is far from private. There are several houses nearby, and a couple of cars have driven past since I stopped in front of the bunker. I don't care. I drop my pack by the door and pull out a paint stick. As quickly as I can, I throw up an outline of the rose, big enough that it fills in the door almost from edge to edge. Then I pull out my light-blue spray can and get to work.

It feels good to be accomplishing something. The smell of aerosol and the way the paint particles rush like tiny blue planets through the thin green glow of the streetlight, the challenge of filling in a tight line with soft, smooth, even color—all of these things blend together in a way that makes me feel totally alive.

I add dark-blue highlights. Then I fill in the stem and the thorns with brown and carefully snap a couple of blasts of white into place to help define the petals of the rose. Finally, I gauge my distance and steady my arm and shoot a perfect curl of red into the outlined drop of blood. I snap the cover back onto the spray paint and zip up my pack.

I walk back and stand on the sidewalk, staring at the rose. I can tell right away that it's the best one I've done. The shape is perfect, and the coloring sits right up against the thick black edge. The building, so ugly on its own, has become a perfect neutral frame, and the rose seems almost to float above the flat, drab gray of the industrial door. It'll be painted over soon, I'm sure, but for the moment it's satisfying to know that I've put my mark on this boring, pointless street.

A car comes to a slow rolling stop behind me, and I know without turning around that it's the cop. There's nowhere to go, and honestly, I'm sick of running. I turn around and bend over to look into the passenger window. He stares past me at at the rose, then looks me in the eye and shakes his head slowly. We look at each other for a few long moments. He parks the car and gets out.

"What the hell is wrong with you?" he asks.

"I don't know what you're talking about," I tell him.

"You know exactly what I'm talking about," he says. He takes a step closer, and I back up. A car comes down the street and slows as it passes us, no doubt taking in the show. He turns to look at the car, and for a split second I reconsider making a run for it, but he's taller than me and in decent shape. I know he can catch me. The car accelerates and drives away.

"You're aware that this is municipal property," he says. It's a statement, not a question.

"You mean the sidewalk?" I ask.

"Don't play stupid," he says. "I've had about enough of that from you. This building that you've defaced is a municipal maintenance shed."

"I haven't defaced anything," I say.

"Listen," he says. "I know what you're up to. You can't hide it any longer, and you'll make things a lot easier on yourself if you don't push this any further."

"I haven't done anything," I say, reminding myself to stay as calm as possible. "I haven't done a thing, and you haven't seen me do anything, and you're starting to make me feel very uncomfortable."

He laughs. "Uncomfortable? That's a new one. Hand over the backpack now, or you'll be charged with obstructing a police officer. Then we'll talk about uncomfortable."

I know he's right. He holds his hand out, and I shrug the strap off my shoulder so that it slides down my arm. I catch it before it hits the ground, and for a minute I let it dangle like that, feeling the weight of the spray cans shift in the pack. I hesitate for a moment.

"Come on," he says, gesturing impatiently with his hand. "Give it here."

I'm about to hand him the pack when a bloodcurdling scream comes at us from somewhere nearby.

"Help!" a woman yells at the top of her lungs. She sounds terrified.

We both turn to look down the street as the woman screams out again, sounding even more anguished. "Help me, please! Help!"

The cop turns and looks at me, opens his mouth as if he's going to say something, then jumps into his car. He peels away from the curb, and I'm out of there, running in the opposite direction.

I've turned the corner and am running as fast as I can when a car squeals up alongside me and the back door opens.

"Get in!" someone calls out.

ANDREA

I don't know where to go or what to do. I'm so upset that I'm shaking. Candace's words spin around inside my head. Is she right? Is my whole life run by other people? If she *is* right, what are the alternatives? Am I supposed to deliberately look for some way to screw the system? Am I supposed to shave my head and get a face tattoo and start chaining myself to government buildings?

Obviously I'm not the kind of person Candace would want to be friends with, but that doesn't give her the right to start judging me. It's not like I have any big desire to hang out with her either. I don't even know where the hell she came from—she just kind of showed up.

I leave Roemi's driveway not knowing where to go or what to do. I begin to walk in the direction of my house, but halfway there I change my mind and start walking in the opposite direction.

I finally get tired of walking aimlessly and sit down on the steps of a church.

I check my watch and realize that the doors to the prom are going to be locked soon. I should be there. Instead, I'm wandering Granite Ridge by myself, delaying the inevitable major fight with my mother. I wonder suddenly why I haven't heard from Bethanne for the past few hours. Then I remember—I have my ringer turned off.

I pull out my phone and see right away that there are a bunch of texts from Bethanne, at least a dozen missed calls from my mom, and a message from my brother from about a half hour ago: call me right now!!!!!!!

He answers before the first ring ends.

"Where the hell are you?" he asks. I can hear Janelle laughing in the background.

"I'm on South Street," I say. "In front of the Catholic church."

"Don't move," he says. "We'll be there in five."

While I'm waiting, I scroll through Bethanne's texts, which all basically say the same thing. I wish you were here!!!! This is so fun!!!!

Brad and Janelle pull up in his ancient Tercel, and I climb into the backseat.

"Mom is losing her mind!" he says. "We had to convince her not to call the cops. That's why we're out here looking for you."

"Oh god." I put my face in my hands and groan.

"No way," he says. "This is awesome. It's about time you stood up for yourself."

"Well, I guess I'll find out if it was worth it when I get home."

"What happened to you anyway?" he asks. "Where have you been?"

"It doesn't matter," I tell them. "I was just about to go home anyway. Can you drive me?"

"I've got a better idea," he says. He grabs his phone from between the front seats and makes a call.

"Dad, it's me," he says after a second. "Put Mom on the phone."

"What are you doing?" I ask him.

He puts a finger to his lips. "Hey, Mom, how's it going?" he says. I can hear her raised voice on the other end of the line, but I can't make out what she's saying.

"Relax," he tells her. "We found her. She's with us now." Her voice drops off on the other end for a split second, then starts up again, even louder.

"No," he says. "I'm not taking her home. She's going to hang out with me and Janelle for a little while. We need to stop at a strip club and pick up some drugs."

Janelle snorts and slaps her hand over her mouth to keep from laughing.

"No, you can't talk to her," says Brad. "She's fine. She's just really drunk, and she's making out with some old guy in the backseat. I didn't quite catch his name—I think it's Larry. I'll ask him when they stop sucking face. He seems nice. Anyway, Mom, I should go. We'll take care of Andrea. You and Dad go to bed. We won't keep her out too late."

He hangs up, and Janelle bursts out laughing. I'm more horrified than amused.

"I don't know how you can talk to her like that," I tell him.

"He's pretty ballsy," says Janelle, grabbing him by the hand. I love Janelle, but sometimes she and Brad take it a bit far with the PDA.

"Mom is just the kind of person who responds well to pushback," says Brad.

"I'm not very good at pushback," I say.

"Maybe not most of the time," he says. "But you sure pushed back tonight. I love it."

"She's going to keep me locked up forever," I tell them.

"She was pretty furious," says Janelle. "I've never seen her that mad."

"That's because you weren't around when I was in high school," says Brad. "You think she's mad tonight? This is nothing."

He's probably right about that. Things were pretty chaotic in our house when Brad was still living at home. I remember lots of knock-down, drag-out fights. Brad coming home drunk and puking in the hallway. Brad being brought to the front door by the cops. Mom finding a giant bag of marijuana in his bedroom. I remember weeks when he wouldn't talk to our parents. He'd get in trouble and they'd lay down new ground rules and he'd just ignore them, coming and going as he pleased. I remember Mom crying a lot.

"It was pretty bad sometimes," I agree.

"Yeah, it was," he says. "I was an asshole." He turns around to look at me. "It's probably my fault that she's so strict with you," he says. "If I hadn't been such a dick, maybe she wouldn't be so scared that you'll turn out the same way."

"You turned out fine!" I say.

"Yeah," he says. "By the skin of my teeth. Thanks to this beautiful woman here." He leans over and kisses Janelle. Good grief.

He looks at me again.

"So what now?" he asks.

"I don't know," I tell him. "It's not like there's anything left to do. I have to go home eventually."

"Yeah, but not yet," he says. "Why don't we go grab something to eat at Bizzby's? You must be starving."

"I am pretty hungry," I agree.

Brad cuts through some back streets on our way toward the strip. We turn a corner and come upon a police cruiser with its lights on. The cop is standing beside the car, talking to someone. I glance out the window.

"Brad, slow down for a second," I say.

It's Candace, and she's obviously in trouble.

"Oh no," I say.

"What's the matter?" asks Brad. The cop turns to look at us, and Brad steps on the gas.

"Do you know that girl?" asks Janelle.

"Yeah," I say. "She's a friend, kind of."

"Doesn't look like someone you'd be friends with," says Brad.

"Not friends, exactly," I say. "We just hung out for a while."

"Well, it looks like your not-exactly friend has got herself wrapped up with the cops," he says.

"She does graffiti," I tell them. "She almost got busted earlier. I think the cop has been watching for her."

I don't know why I even care. Candace was a total bitch to me, but seeing her there, getting grilled, I know she's about to find herself in deep shit. I almost hate to admit it, but I can kind of see her point about being oppressed by society or whatever. I mean, all she did was paint a rose on a concrete building. Who cares? What's going to happen to her now?

"Well, we can't leave her hanging," says Brad, turning a corner and pulling over.

"What should we do?" I ask.

He turns to Janelle. "You up for a bit of acting practice?"

The minute she's out of the car, Janelle runs to a tree, hides behind it and begins screaming. As we drive away, we can hear her clear as a bell from the open windows of the car. I hope this works, because it won't

be long till neighbors start coming out of their houses
to see what's wrong.

Brad takes a corner fast and then we see Candace,
running along the sidewalk.

"There she is," I shout, and Brad comes to a squealing
halt.

I open the back door and stick my head out. "Get in!"
I yell.

When she sees me, her mouth drops open, but she
jumps into the car.

"What the hell is going on?" she demands.

"You're welcome," says Brad.

"Better get down," I tell her. She crouches as low as
she can.

Brad drives back the way we came until we see Janelle
walking down the sidewalk toward us. The police car is
nowhere in sight. Brad pulls over, and Janelle pops back
into the front seat.

"That was easy!" she says as we drive away.

"How did it go down?" asks Brad.

"I just screamed until I saw the cop car coming, and
then I started strolling. I don't think he even glanced at
me as he drove by."

"That was you screaming?" asks Candace. "I don't
understand."

"Janelle's an actress," I tell her.

"Just a bit of theater," says Janelle.

"Wait a minute," says Candace. "You guys planned this? To help me?"

She looks at me and I shrug. "We couldn't just leave you there."

"It was fun," says Janelle, turning around to smile at Candace.

Candace's mouth opens and closes several times. "Thank you," she finally manages to get out.

"Don't mention it," says Brad. "A not-exactly friend of Andrea's is a not-exactly friend of mine."

"What happened to Paul and Roemi?" I ask.

"I don't even know, really," she says. "It was kind of crazy. Roemi wanted to drive past the prom, and then we ran into some messed-up friend of Paul's and he talked a bunch of shit to Roemi."

"Was his name Penner?" I ask.

"That's the guy," she says. "Anyway, Roemi took off for home, and I left Paul behind at the dance."

I groan. "Penner's such a jerk. Do you think we should go see if Roemi's okay?" I ask.

She considers. "You know what?" she says. "That's not such a bad idea."

PAUL

It would be impossible to feel more like a piece of shit than I do. I consider getting out of the Cruiser and chasing after Candace, but something tells me she's not interested in talking to me. So I just sit there for a few minutes, watching, as Penner walks back to the school and joins the last of the stragglers. Mr. Parrins, one of the gym teachers, is holding the front door open, ushering them inside. He follows them in and pulls the heavy door closed behind him.

I know the first thing Penner is going to do is find Lannie and tell her what just happened. I imagine her inside the dance, her night already ruined, and now about to learn that I lied to her. That her big night is messed up because I choked. Because I'm weak and can't even control my own emotions.

Candace hit the nail on the head. I am a poser.

The only people who really knew me aren't around anymore, and that's my fault too. When I was friends with Jerry and Ahmed, maybe we were a bunch of losers, but even if we were, we either didn't know or didn't care. We spent every spare minute together, just hanging out. Shooting hoops in Ahmed's driveway. Talking about girls.

I remember one night at Jerry's house when I was about fourteen. I'd stayed over, and I was lying in bed thinking about my grandfather. He'd had a heart attack and died a few weeks earlier, totally unexpectedly. I started having a panic attack. Jerry woke up, and somehow he talked me down, and we stayed up all night. Playing video games. Talking about death and the universe and all that deep shit. He knew what was going on with me. He didn't laugh at me. Now I don't even have any time for the guy. We're still cool on the surface, but it's not the same.

When Lannie and I started to go out, Jerry and Ahmed were happier for me than anybody. Look how that turned out.

And then it occurs to me. Whoever I am, or whoever I was, nobody really knows that person. I don't even think I can describe him to myself. My breath becomes shallow. My head starts to tighten. I should have known better. I thought the anxiety was gone, but it was just hiding.

I sit like this for a while, feeling as if I'm circling a whirlpool, knowing that if I'm not careful, I'll get sucked right down into the negative space and then who knows what will happen. But it's knowing this, realizing that I'm circling, that I'm still up on the edge, that gives me the push to start breathing deeply. Deep, slow breaths. In and out. In and out. In and out.

After a while, it's okay. I'm not even sure exactly how much time has passed, but the music is still thudding inside the school gym. A little bit of every note and every beat escapes through the concrete wall, and soft rhythmic waves float through the air and dissolve around me as I sit in Roemi's parents' suv.

I open the door and get out. I stretch and then stroll down the road a little bit. I'm relieved that I was able to push through the attack, but I need to start moving so it doesn't happen again. I turn back toward the Land Cruiser and look at the ladder carefully strapped to the ski rack. I might as well take care of business.

Mom's car is in the driveway when I get home. I try to make as little noise as possible as I take the ladder off the top of the suv. I open the door to the front porch and grab Dad's keys, then somehow manage to get the ladder into the truck by myself. When I walk back around the side of the house, my mother is sitting on the front stoop, looking at me.

"Hey," I say.

"Hey yourself," she says. "Nice ride." She gestures at the Cruiser.

"Yeah, it's not bad," I say.

"Anything I need to know or hear about?" she asks.

"Nah," I say.

"Fair enough."

"I've got to take this back," I say. "It belongs to a friend. I didn't steal it, I promise."

She smiles. "I didn't think you did. Are you having an okay night?"

"Yeah," I say.

"I don't believe you. You feeling okay?"

"Yeah, I feel fine." I just stand there, looking at the ground.

She pats the step next to her. "Come on and sit down for a minute."

I sit next to her, then lean forward and put my face in my hands. She reaches over and rubs my back.

"You're going to be okay," she says. "You were okay before, and you'll be okay again."

I nod. For a few minutes we just sit there, not saying anything.

"I did something stupid," I say after a while. "I did something to one of my friends, and now I regret it."

"Well," she says. "Maybe you should fix it."

*   *   *

I park in the circular turning spot at Roemi's house. I walk to the front door, and for a second I consider just dropping the keys in the mailbox and leaving. Instead, I force myself to reach out and ring the doorbell.

The door opens and Roemi's mother smiles at me.

"Hello," she says.

"Hi," I say. "I'm, um, one of Roemi's friends."

"Yes," she says. "You're not Roemi's boyfriend."

"That's right. Is he home? Roemi, I mean?"

I hear a door open at the top of the landing and look up to see Roemi poking his head out of his bedroom.

"Roemi," his mother calls up to him. "Your friend is here."

Roemi squints at me suspiciously, then sticks his head back into his room and says something to someone. The door opens wider, and Candace and Andrea come out of the room behind him. Andrea looks surprised to see me. Candace looks pissed. As usual.

Roemi doesn't move to come downstairs. He just stands at the top of the staircase and crosses his arms.

"Hey, guys," I say. Andrea raises her hand to wave at me, but Candace and Roemi don't say anything.

Roemi's father comes out into the hallway.

"I was getting a bit worried," he says. "It was very irresponsible of Roemi to leave without making sure the Land Cruiser got home safe and sound." He turns and looks up the stairs at Roemi. "Wasn't it, Roemi?"

"Dad, I *told* you, it's very complicated!"

"He's right," I say. "It's my fault. I'm sorry."

"Well, we won't worry about it now," he says. "How did you find the ride?"

"Oh man," I say. "It was really nice. Really smooth."

"Yes, there's a lot of power under that hood," he says.

"Oh yeah," I say. "I'd love to see how she handles offroad."

"Dad!" says Roemi. "We are angry at Paul."

"I'm not angry at Paul," says Roemi's dad.

"Well, I am!" he yells.

"Roemi," I say, "I'm sorry. I shouldn't have let Penner talk about you like that."

"And?"

"And I really appreciate that you helped me out with your parents' Land Cruiser."

"And?"

"Thank you for distracting Lannie's mom by tap-dancing at Starbucks."

"And?"

"I don't know what you want me to say," I tell him. "I'm really sorry, and thank you."

"Aren't you going to tell me how nice I look in my tuxedo?"

I laugh. "Can you guys come down here for a minute? I have an idea."

I turn to Roemi's dad. "I wonder if you'd be willing to let us borrow the Land Cruiser for a little while longer, sir."

"That depends," he says. "Is it very important?"

"It is," I say. "It couldn't be more important."

He considers for a moment.

"Well, in that case," he says, "why don't you take the Audi?"

ROEMI

I have to hand it to Paul: he's gone from homophobia enabler to gay-love coach in about half an hour. At first I think it's some kind of weird joke when he tells me that we should drive into the city and confront John, but he sounds sincere, and I can't think of any reason not to believe him.

After mulling it over for, like, ten seconds, I begin to see the romantic potential in the whole scenario. Maybe John will be so excited to see me that we'll make out right there in the middle of the street in front of his house, and then his parents will stand in the doorway and be so touched by our love that they'll give our relationship their full blessing, and then Paul will drive us back to town and we'll kidnap Ryan Penner and duct-tape his fat bigoted ass to a telephone pole, and then Candace will spray-paint something hilarious all over him, and then we'll skid triumphantly to a stop in front of the school and everyone at the prom will come streaming outside to see what the commotion is, and then we'll have a huge flash-mob dance-o-rama in the parking lot.

At the very least, I'll get to meet the guy in person for the first time.

Paul looks like he's going to poop his pants when Dad hands him the keys to the Audi. We sit in the garage for a minute as he caresses the steering wheel. Then he turns the key, revs the engine and pulls out into the street. Before we know it, we're flying down the highway and into the city.

"You sure you know where he lives?" asks Andrea.

"Thirty-two Weldon Street," I say without hesitating. "I've Google-Street-Viewed the shit out of that place."

"All right," says Paul. "Here goes nothing."

Candace knows the area, so she directs Paul to a residential neighborhood. We turn onto John's street and all of a sudden we're there, sitting in front of his house.

"What now?" I ask.

"What do you mean, *what now*?" says Andrea. "Go up and ring the doorbell. Ask for John. Tell him what you think."

"I don't know what I think," I say. It's true. Now that we're here, and I'm going to see the first guy I almost dated, I don't know what I think about it. Maybe Andrea was right earlier. Maybe I don't really know anything about this guy.

Candace leans in from the backseat. "Roemi, this is no time to be a chickenshit."

"Sorry," I say. "I am a chickenshit. I can't do it. One of you has to go up and see if he's home."

"I'll go," says Andrea. "I don't mind talking to him. I'll get him to meet you around the corner or something."

She jumps out of the car, and we watch her run up and ring the doorbell. After a minute, a man I assume is John's dad opens the front door. Andrea talks to him briefly, and then he closes the door and she runs back to the car.

"He's not home," she says.

"Where is he?" I ask.

"His dad doesn't know. Out with friends somewhere."

I feel kind of relieved and totally crushed at the same time.

"Well, that's that, I guess," I say.

"What are we going to do now?" asks Paul. He looks at me. "You get to choose, man. Whatever you want."

I think for a second.

"Do they have a Bizzby's here?"

"You have got to be kidding me," says Candace, but she's laughing.

* * *

It amazes me how everything looks much the same whether you're in a suburb or a small town or a city. There's always a stretch of street with a Starbucks and a Walmart and a bunch of fast-food places. Bizzby's diners are popping up everywhere, like mushrooms. We cruise down a street lined with shops and restaurants; if you squinted, you'd swear you were driving along the strip in Granite Ridge. Or San Francisco, or Winnipeg. Stick some onion domes on top of those suckers and you could be in Moscow.

Andrea points out a Bizzby's, and we pull into the parking lot. Just as we're about to get out of the car, I say, "Stop."

"What's the deal?" asks Paul.

"That's him," I say, staring through Bizzby's big plate-glass window. "That's John."

He's in a booth with two girls. They're all laughing about something, and it looks like I'm the last thing on his mind. My heart sinks. What else did I expect? The guy stood me up.

"Oh, he's just doing a great job of pretending to be straight," I say. "They're probably sharing a banana split and talking about *Glee*." I try to sound like I don't care, but my heart is pounding and my mouth is dry. I wonder if he knows how excited I was about tonight. I stare at him through the window, trying to make out what he's saying. He looks happy, which pisses me off. I'm aware of Paul and Candace and Andrea looking at me, waiting for me to make a move.

"Let's go," I say finally.

"What? No way, man," says Paul. He reaches over, grabs me by the shoulder and shakes me. "We found him, Roemi! We can't just turn around and leave."

"What good is it going to do?" I ask. "What's the point? He's obviously happier hanging out with his stupid friends here at Bizzby's—which, I should add, is *my* favorite place in the world, *not his*!"

"Roemi," says Andrea, "calm down. I'm going to get him out here."

"No, don't!" I say. "None of his friends know he's gay! I'm pissed at the guy, but I don't want to *out* him!"

"Don't worry," she says. "I won't out anyone."

I watch helplessly as she walks up to the door and goes into the restaurant. Through the window, I see her walk right up to John's booth. He and his friends look up as she speaks. My heart starts to pound again as he gets up and follows her outside. Then he's beside the Audi, and Andrea is opening the back door.

He bends down to look past her into the car, the curious look on his face turning quickly to confusion when he sees me.

"What's going on?" he asks.

I can't think of anything to say. He looks totally freaked out, although he doesn't move.

"Hey," says Candace, sticking out her hand to him. "I'm Candace, and this is Paul. You obviously know Roemi. Why don't you get in?"

He hesitates, then quickly turns to look back through the restaurant window. His friends are busy talking, not paying any attention to us. He hesitates again, then climbs into the backseat. Andrea follows and closes the door behind them. Crammed between Candace and Andrea, John looks like he'd rather be anywhere else on earth.

"Okay, what's happening?" he asks, looking right at me. "What are you doing here?"

Now that we're face to face, I can't think of what to say. This seemed like such a good idea when Paul suggested it, but it's just really awful and awkward. All the scathingly witty things that I've been working out in my mind evaporate. The car fills with a dense, uncomfortable silence. Then Paul speaks up, turning around to look John in the eye.

"We're Roemi's friends, and we wanted to help him find out why you ditched him tonight."

"This is really weird," says John. "I—this is—how am I supposed to talk to you with a bunch of people here?"

"I think there's a park around the corner," says Candace. "Why don't you guys go over there for some privacy?"

"I don't know. I don't think this is a good idea," he says.

Finally, I find my voice. "Good idea?" I say. "Here's a bad idea for you. How about standing me up on the biggest night of my life? Do you see this tux? This cost a lot of money to rent. I had *everything* planned!"

"Fine," he says, sighing. "Let's go."

We get out of the car and walk around the corner and into a little park with a playground. I follow him to a swing set and take a seat. Neither of us says anything for a minute. We just sit there, floating above the sand. Kicking our feet.

"What do you want to ask me?" he finally says.

"Why did you do this?" I ask him. "Why did you lead me on and then just drop me like that?"

"Okay, wait a minute," he says. "I didn't lead you on. You dragged me along, and then I freaked out at the last minute. I didn't know how to tell you how I felt, and every time I tried, you brushed me off and hijacked the conversation with prom talk."

"But you sounded like you wanted to come!" I say.

"I did," he says. "Or at least, I thought I did. The idea of it sounded kind of fun. You made being gay sound so easy, and I started to think I could do it—I mean, I liked thinking that I could just be myself."

"You *can* be yourself!" I say. "Look at me!"

"You don't get it, Roemi," he says. "My parents are super religious. When my sister got a tattoo, they freaked out. Grounded her for weeks. I can't risk them finding out about me—not now, not while I'm still living with them. It's easy for you, and I admire that, but it isn't easy for me."

"You think it's easy for me?" I say. "You think I just roll through life without any hassle? I'm the only out gay kid at my school. Tonight I had garbage thrown at me from a moving car, and I was called names by at least two people. You think that's easy?"

He looks at me sadly. "Don't you understand? That's why I'm so afraid."

"Well, it's better to be yourself and be afraid than to hide and be afraid," I snap.

"Maybe," he says.

"You really hurt my feelings," I say after a minute. My voice cracks a little bit, and I think I might start crying. I don't care. I want him to feel bad.

"I know," he says. "I should have said something to you. I'm really sorry. I really do like talking to you online. I was starting to build up the nerve to actually meet you, go for coffee or something, and then you sprang this prom thing on me. I'm not ready for that, Roemi."

"I'm sorry," I tell him.

"Don't apologize," he says. "I'm the one who should be sorry for ruining your night." He gets off the swing. "I should get back," he says. "Are we cool?"

This isn't what I expected. I thought we were going to have a big romantic moment, but instead I'm getting ditched for the second time in one night.

"We're cool," I say finally. But I can't look at him. I can feel him staring at me. Then he walks away.

I dangle in the swing for a few more minutes before I get off and walk back to the car.

ANDREA

When Roemi gets back, he isn't very happy.

"Tonight is the worst," he says.

"It could always be worse," says Paul.

"How?" asks Roemi. "My date's a dickhead, your friend is an asshole, Andrea's mom is a bitch, and Candace is on the lam."

There's not much to say to that. He definitely has a point.

Then something occurs to me. "Do you know how to get to the university from here?" I ask Candace.

"Yeah," she says. "My mom works there. Why?"

"There's something I want to show you guys," I tell them.

Classes are out for the summer, so when we drive onto the campus most of the buildings are dark and the place looks deserted.

We go to the meal hall, a one-story building attached to one of the dormitories. Paul pulls the Audi onto a gravel maintenance road behind it and parks in the shadow between some outbuildings.

"Over here," I tell them. I lead the way, climbing up onto a Dumpster, hopping across to the top of a small porch and then hoisting myself over the edge and onto the roof of the building. The roof is covered with gravel, and there's a three-foot-wide ledge running along three sides. On the fourth side, the dorm building rises up three stories higher, and a brick wall studded with windows and a fire-escape ladder looks down on where I'm standing.

"This is crazy," says Paul once we're all on the roof. "How did you know about this place?"

"I went to a science camp here a couple of years ago," I tell them. "You think *I'm* a nerd? You should have seen some of those girls. Anyway, one night some of us snuck out of our dorm and managed to climb up here."

"Andrea Feingold, the original badass," says Roemi.

"Not exactly," I say. "We were looking for somewhere to do an experiment. See, we'd been trying to prove whether—"

"Please stop," says Roemi. "Don't destroy the moment."

We walk to the front of the building and look out past the university campus. This view is what I remember most clearly about that night. The university is built at the top of a parklike slope. The downtown stretches to our right, and ahead of us, in the distance, we can see the lights of Granite Ridge, sitting like an island in the darkness beyond the city.

"It looks so small from here," says Paul.

"It is small," says Roemi. "Too small for us. I can't wait to get out."

"Man," says Paul. "I wouldn't want to get out if I lived in a house like yours."

"Yeah, but it's not like I'm going to live with my parents forever," says Roemi. "I'm getting the hell away from Granite Ridge as soon as humanly possible. I want to make it big, in a *real* city. Where I can actually date guys and live without worrying about people calling me names or wanting to beat me up."

"I'm not going to hang out with Penner anymore," Paul announces. "Seriously, I mean it," he says when we all turn to look at him.

"Won't Lannie have something to say about that?" asks Roemi.

"Lannie doesn't choose my friends for me," says Paul. "I mean, it's not like she said 'stop hanging out with your friends and only hang out with me and my friends.'"

"That's kind of what happened though, isn't it?" I ask him.

"Yeah," he says. "But it just kind of worked out that way. Lannie and Darrah have been best friends forever, so Penner is always around."

"What about Jerry and Ahmed though?" I ask. "You guys have been friends forever too, but it seems like you never hang out with them anymore."

"Yeah," he says. "I know. That's totally my fault. But I'm serious. I'm going to stop hanging out with him. I never liked the guy anyway. Tomorrow I'm going to tell Lannie how I feel."

Candace walks away from us and stares up at the side of the dormitory.

"This is really great," she says, pointing at a large blank space in the middle of the wall, cornered by four windows. "I can totally do something up there."

She throws her pack over her shoulder and starts climbing the fire-escape ladder. When she's about eight rungs up, she stops. The rest of us watch as she pulls a black paint stick from the front pocket of her pack. With one hand on the ladder, she swings out from the wall and sizes it up. Then she pulls herself back in, hooks an arm around one of the rungs and stretches sideways, reaching as far as she can with the paint stick. She's just about to start drawing when Paul says, "Shit! Candace, get down!"

She turns, confused, as a window to her right slides open. A red-faced woman sticks her head out and cranes her neck, staring at Candace.

"What are you doing?" the woman yells. She looks down, and her mouth drops open when she sees the rest of us. Her face disappears inside the building.

"Security!" yells Paul. "Hurry up!"

Candace scurries down the ladder, jumping from the fourth rung and landing in a crouch. We rush to the edge of the building and climb over the edge, one at a time. I hit the ground first.

"Andrea!" Paul yells. I look up at him, and he tosses me the keys to the car. "Get her started!"

I jump into the car, turn it on and pull it over by the Dumpster. Roemi jumps into the front passenger seat as Candace and then Paul hop to the ground and dive into the backseat. The security guard comes running around the side of the building and stops about twenty feet in front of us, right in the middle of the maintenance road. Our exit is totally blocked. She throws her hand up toward us, as if she's trying to cast a spell.

"Stop!" she yells.

"Flash the brights on and off, really quick!" says Roemi.

I do what he says, and the guard stumbles back and throws her arm over her eyes to block the light.

"Go!" yells Paul.

"I can't! She's blocking us!" I say, still flicking the lights as the guard gets her bearings and comes lumbering toward us.

"Back it up!" Paul hollers.

I throw the car into reverse and glance quickly over my shoulder. On a hill covered with large oak trees is a narrow walking path that looks just wide enough for the car.

I aim for it and step on the gas. The Audi guns up the hill in reverse. At the top, I quickly snap it into Drive and we spin around the side of the building, over a lawn and onto a paved road.

"That way," says Candace, pointing at a side road. "It leads off campus!"

In the rearview mirror, I see the security guard running along the lawn behind us, but I take the turn and we lose her. I race toward the university exit, drive through the open gate and turn onto a quiet residential street. Candace points the way and I follow her directions, my heart pounding as we move deeper into the city. Finally, after we've turned onto a busy street, Candace points at a parking space in front of a condo building.

"Pull in here," she says.

I roll up next to the curb, turn off the ignition and carefully remove my shaking hands from the steering wheel.

"I think I just pooped a little," says Roemi.

"Andrea, that was some rock-star driving back there," says Paul.

"Well, I don't feel like a rock star. I feel like a criminal or something."

"Relax," says Candace, "everything's cool. No cops around. I doubt that woman got the license plate. Pretty smooth move, flashing the lights at her."

"I saw that on *CSI*," says Roemi.

"Okay," says Candace. "Let's go." She opens her door and gets out of the car. When none of us move, she bends over and looks in at us.

"What are you waiting for?"

CANDACE

When my dad moved out, my mother went kind of crazy and threw out everything that reminded her of their lives together. She told me it was a way of bringing fresh energy into our house. When that didn't work, she sold the house and we moved into a condo downtown. The condo is okay, but I'm not in love with it or anything. It's too new to consider home.

Mom's out of town with her boyfriend Walter for the weekend, which works out well.

"Come on in," I say, snapping on the lights. "Grab a seat. I need to find something."

I go into my mother's bedroom, trying to ignore Walter's boxers lying on the floor. I rummage around in her closet for a few minutes until I find something I think might work and bring it back to the kitchen.

"Here," I say, thrusting it at Andrea.

"What is this?" she asks.

"It's a dress," I tell her. "It's my mom's. You're about her size."

"I don't understand," she says.

"Isn't it obvious?" asks Roemi. "She hates your clothes."

"No," I say. "I think you should go to prom. You too," I say to Roemi.

"Oh my god, Andrea," says Roemi. "It's, like, destiny! We have to crash the prom. We can be each other's date!"

"Roemi," she says, "the prom will be over soon. It's not gonna happen."

"Well, we'd better get a move on," he says. "Come on, girl. Just try the dress on."

She thinks about it for a minute, then stands up. "Where's the bathroom?"

"Come with me," I tell her.

She follows me into my room, and I point her to the bathroom in the corner.

"What do you think?" she asks when she comes out a few minutes later.

"It looks great," I tell her. It does look great. She's wearing what my mother refers to as her *little black cocktail dress*. Nothing fancy, just a black slip with spaghetti straps.

"We need to do something about your hair though," I say.

I reach up and push my hands into her hair, then start tousling it.

"This doesn't feel like an improvement," she says.

"Just give me a minute," I tell her. There's a black button-up shirt hanging on the back of my bedroom door. I grab it and get some scissors from my desk and begin to cut an inch-wide strip from the lower hem of the shirt.

"Oh my god," she says. "What are you doing?"

"Don't worry about it," I say. "Sometimes you gotta break some eggs if you want to make an omelette."

I twist the fabric in and around her hair. Soon her hair is up off her neck, and it actually looks really good. I loosen a few strands so they fall off to the side of her face.

"We're not quite done," I say. "Grab a seat."

I dig around for a few minutes in the messy depths of my closet. "Here we go," I say, pulling a small knapsack out from behind a cardboard box full of old shoes. I dump the bag, which is full of makeup, out on the desk. Then I grab some eyeliner and pull the chair from my desk over to sit in front of her.

"Close your eyes and lean back your head," I say.

"Where did you learn to do this?" she asks as I outline her eyes.

"A good friend of mine used to be really into makeup," I say. "I guess she still is. I haven't really talked to her in over a year. She left this stuff here the last time she came over, and she hasn't been back for it. Anyway, she's really good. Taught me a few things."

I pull out a tube of lipstick and open it. Dark red. Perfect. I hand it to Andrea; she puts it on and then smacks her lips together.

"I'm not used to wearing makeup," she says, staring at herself in the mirror. She turns around to look at me. "Thanks," she says. "Seriously."

"Listen," I say. "About all that shit I said before…"

"Forget it," she says.

"No, seriously," I say. "I don't know what made me act like such a bitch. And it was really cool of you and your brother to help me out like that."

"Don't worry about it," she says. "Besides, I had the wrong impression about what it is that you do."

"What do you mean?" I ask.

"I guess I just never thought of graffiti as being… I don't know, artistic. That rose you painted though. It was really beautiful."

"Are you serious?" I say.

"Yeah," she says. "I'll be pissed when they paint it over."

"That might be the nicest thing anyone's said to me in a long time," I tell her. "Okay, turn around. One last thing."

I pull my bag of markers out of my backpack and get her to hold the loose tendrils of her hair up off her neck. I quickly sketch out a rose, but I do it upside down so that the stem and thorns twist up her neck and the

flower sits dead center at the top of her back. Instead
of filling it in with blue, I use a dark red that matches
her lipstick.

When I'm done, I hold a mirror at the back of her
neck so she can see. "Perfect," we say at the same time.

When we go back out to the kitchen, Roemi puts two
fingers in his mouth and gives her a loud jock whistle.

"Wow," says Paul.

"Wow what?" asks Andrea. "Does it look okay?"

"You look awesome," says Roemi. "Justin won't know
what hit him."

"Justin Sanchez?" asks Paul.

"Oops," says Roemi.

"Thanks a lot, Roemi," says Andrea, laughing.

"You guys would be a cool couple," says Paul. "He's a
good guy."

"You think so?" asks Andrea.

"He'll have to get past me," says Roemi. "She's my
date tonight."

"Not so fast," I tell him.

* * *

My school is right downtown and has seen better days.
It's big and brick and rough around the edges. It has a
lot of things going for it, but architectural integrity isn't
one of them.

The sidewalk out front is jammed with people. Smoke from cigarettes and weed sits in the air, and lots of people are openly drinking.

"Prom night at Sodom and Gomorrah High School," says Roemi. "I should have transferred here years ago."

Paul parks across the street.

"Probably best if you guys stay here," I tell them. "I'll be back in ten minutes."

I walk across the street. A few people turn to watch me as I approach, but nobody bothers to talk to me. Not much of a surprise, considering I haven't socialized with any of them in over a year.

I walk up the front steps to the school and into the entry hallway. The doors to the gymnasium sit directly in front of me. Through them, I can see lights spinning across the floor and hear the music pounding at full blast.

Jenny Dervette is standing by herself at the entrance to the gym, staring at her phone, because apparently there aren't enough people here for her to interact with.

"Hey," I say. "Do you know if Sean is here tonight?"

"Yeah," she says, barely glancing up at me. "I've seen him around. I think he's probably dancing."

I walk into the gym and stand on the edge of the dance floor. I see him right away, busting a move with a group of adoring girls. Sean has always been an awesome dancer.

The dance song ends, and as some cheesy ballad starts, the floor more or less empties. It must be too early in the evening for people to start sucking face, although I notice that a few couples are making exceptions. Sean moves toward the other side of the gym, and I push through the crowd, trying to follow him.

Someone steps out of my way, and all of a sudden I'm standing face to face with Vanessa.

She looks as surprised as I am. Her eyes widen, and I can tell that she's struggling to come up with something to say. I'm not, since I don't have anything to say to her at all. I don't move though. I just stand there as we look at each other. It's been months since we've said a word to each other. She's with Evan Wong, who stands to the side and looks back and forth between us, as if he's trying to figure out what to do. Vanessa's always thought Evan is pretty cute. I've seen her in the hallways with him lately and had assumed they're an item now. I guess this proves it.

"I'm going to hit up the bathroom," he tells her before he walks away, leaving us.

"Hey," she says finally.

I feel frozen in place. "You look good," I manage to tell her. It's true. She's got a cool vintage dress on, and she's wearing new glasses, red-framed cat-eyes. Right up her alley.

"Thanks," she says. "I got the dress online. I was pretty excited when I found it."

"Yeah, you look good," I say again. I feel incredibly stupid and begin to walk away, but she reaches out and grabs my arm.

"Candace," she says. "What is going on?"

"I'm trying to do a favor for a friend," I tell her.

"No, I mean, what's going on with us? What happened?"

"Oh give me a break," I say, feeling my face getting hot. "You know what happened. You ratted me out." I realize my voice is raised and people are looking at us, so I lean in and lower it. "You called my *mother*, Vanessa. How could you do that?"

"Candace, I was worried about you! You changed so much, so quick. It freaked me out, and then when you and Rick…"

"You were jealous of him," I say. "You were jealous that I'd found something special in my life, and you didn't understand it, so you had to ruin it."

She snorts. "Special? You mean breaking into buildings just to impress some guy who treated you like shit?"

"He didn't treat me like shit," I tell her.

"Oh yeah? So where is awesome Rick now?" she asks. "How come he's not here with you tonight?"

I laugh at her. "I should have known you'd bring that up. You're just thrilled to have that to fall back on, aren't you?"

"Jesus, Candace," she says. "Do you even understand why you're so angry at everyone? Do you even think about it?"

"There's nothing to think about," I tell her. "It's all pretty straightforward."

"You really see things that way, don't you?" she asks. "It's just you against the world."

"That sure is how things turned out," I say.

She stares at me. "I don't know what happened, Candace," she says finally. "I miss you."

"Shit," I say. I put my hand up to cover my face and squeeze my temples. "Vanessa, I miss you too. We're just too different now."

"Too different for what?" she asks me. "To be friends? Do you really think that?"

"I don't know," I say. "I don't know what I think anymore." To my horror, I feel my eyes start to well up.

"Oh, Candace," she says, reaching out to put a hand on my shoulder. "I'm still here, if you ever decide you want me around."

She turns and walks away. For a split second I want to follow her, grab her and tell her that I'm sorry, but the moment passes. I watch her move away through the crowd.

I spot Sean sitting on the stage, talking to a couple of girls. All I want to do is get out of here as quickly as possible, so I walk over to them and interrupt one of the girls in mid-sentence.

"Hey, Sean," I say. "Do you have a second?"

"Candace," he says, surprised. "What's up?"

"Do you have a date tonight?" I ask him.

ROEMI

When Candace comes back to the car, she's with some guy. He's totally cute, average height but nicely built, with cropped ginger hair and a killer smile. He's also super well dressed, in a tailored gray suit jacket over a white shirt with the top couple of buttons undone, dark pants and electric-blue Chuck Taylors.

They climb into the backseat, and the new dude smiles at us.

"Everyone," says Candace, "this is Sean. Sean, this is everyone."

I wonder if he's her not-quite boyfriend or what, but then he leans into the front seat and holds his hand out to me. "Hey," he says. "You must be Roemi."

"Yes," I say. "I must be."

There's an awkward moment in which it dawns on me that Sean is some kind of blind date. I twist my head around to look at Candace.

"Hey, man," she says. "You're the one who wanted to be the first gay prom couple in Granite Ridge."

"So you grabbed the first gay person you could find and just assumed that would work?" I ask her.

"Hey," she says. "Sean's a friend of mine, and I happen to think you guys might hit it off."

I turn to Sean. "You're sure you're cool with this?" I ask him. "You don't mind leaving your own prom to come with us?"

"No way," he says. "It's pretty dead in there."

"I wouldn't get my hopes up," I tell him, looking out the window at the crowd outside the school. "This is probably like an all-night rave on Ibiza compared to ours."

"No worries," he says. "At least I have a date now."

He smiles at me, and I feel like I'm going to melt into the upholstery.

"Okay, Paul," I say. "We have less than an hour of prom left. Let's gun it."

"If you insist," says Paul, revving the engine and pulling away from the curb.

We make it back to Granite Ridge in record time. Paul parks on the far side of the sports field behind the school. We get out of the car and stand, facing the building. From across the field, we can hear the faint thump of heavy bass coming from the gymnasium.

"I guess this is it," says Andrea.

"You sure you don't want to come with us?" I ask Paul. "There's still time to salvage Lannie's prom."

"I don't think I'll be salvaging anything if I show up at the end of the night in jeans and a ballcap," he says. "You guys go ahead. I'll stick around and drive everyone home after the dance."

"You'll be here?" I ask Candace.

"Where else would I go?" she asks.

"All right then." I turn to Andrea and Sean. "What are we waiting for?"

The three of us step onto the field and start walking toward the school.

"How do you know Candace?" Andrea asks Sean.

"We have some of the same friends," he says. "Or used to anyway. Nobody's seen much of Candace over the last year or so. I was surprised when she came looking for me tonight, actually."

"I'm glad she did," I say, feeling embarrassed the minute the words are out of my mouth. It takes a lot to make me blush, but I can feel color rising in my cheeks.

Sean doesn't seem to notice. "Me too," he says. "Totally glad."

From the corner of my eye, I see Andrea grin.

When we reach the far side of the field, we stand on the edge of the parking lot and look at the school. The music is a lot louder now, and I can make out a Beyoncé song through the heavy walls of the gym.

"Maybe this isn't such a great idea," says Andrea. "We'll never get in."

"Leave it to me," I say. She and Sean follow me to the side of the school, and we creep up to the corner and peek around it. Through the glass walls of the school foyer, we can see a bunch of teachers milling around inside, up past their bedtimes.

"We aren't going to make it in that way," I tell them.

Andrea opens her mouth to say something, but I hold my finger up. "Hush," I say. "Just follow me."

We walk around to the back of the building, trying doors as we go. Everything is locked.

Then I look up and see an open window that's hinged inward. The only problem is that it's five feet off the ground.

"I think that's the bio lab," Andrea says. "I don't know—that opening is really small."

"Come on, Andrea," I say. "We've made it this far. Just think about the great story this will make!"

"I wish we still had that stupid ladder," she mutters.

It takes a bit of maneuvering, but Sean and I manage to hoist her up to the window.

"Can you see anything?" Sean asks.

"It's dark," she says. "Give me a second."

"Well, hurry—you aren't as featherlight as you look!" I say.

"Okay," she says. "There's a counter here, just below the window. I'm going to try to climb in."

I give her one last shove, and then she's hanging half in and half out of the window. With a little yelp, she falls into the building. We hear a crash, then some cursing, and a moment later she sticks her head out the window. "I'm okay," she says. "I just knocked a bunch of papers and stuff onto the floor. It's clear. There's nobody around."

I turn to Sean, who has been taking everything in stride.

"Maybe you can help me up next," I say.

"Sure thing," he says. "This is super fun."

"You mean it?" I ask him.

"Definitely," he says.

Sean makes a step out of his hands, and I grab on to his shoulders. Our faces are suddenly very close, and we stay like that, staring at each other, for a split second. Then we both burst out laughing, and he boosts me up to the window. Once I'm inside, Andrea and I reach down and grab on to his arms to pull him up.

The room is dark. I hop off the counter and go over to the door; I peer through the window into the dimly lit hallway.

"The coast is clear," I whisper to them. "Let's clean this mess up and get the hell out of here."

We begin picking up papers from the floor and trying to rearrange them as neatly as possible. I'm about to climb back onto the counter and shut the window when the door is thrown open and the light snaps on.

It's Mr. Parrins, and he doesn't look happy.

"What the hell are you guys doing in here?" he asks. None of us answer, and he walks into the room. He looks at the window, which is open twice as wide as it should be, and then the counter, which is in total disarray despite our best efforts.

"All right," says Mr. Parrins. "You kids are coming with me."

"Mr. Parrins," I say. "You can't do this to us!"

"Do what?" he asks, obviously impatient.

"You can't ruin tonight for us, and if you had any idea the trouble we went through to get here, you wouldn't try!"

"Roemi, there are rules," he says. "One of the rules is that the doors to the dance are closed and locked at ten thirty. An even more important rule is not to break into the school. Or any building, for that matter."

"Don't you see what's going on here?" I ask him. "This is my date, Sean. Do you get what I'm saying here? Do you realize that if you let us into the dance we'll be the first gay couple to ever attend prom at Granite Ridge High School?"

"Actually," says Mr. Parrins, "you won't be. Allison Jackson and her girlfriend were the first. About five years ago. The paper did a really nice write-up about it."

Five years ago?

"Excuse me?" I say. "You mean we aren't the first gay couple to come to the prom?"

"That's what I said," he says. "Although technically, as far as I know, you'd be the first gay male couple to attend prom."

"Technically," I repeat.

"Anyway, it doesn't matter," says Mr. Parrins. "Gay, straight, whatever. You've broken into the school—don't you understand how serious that is? You guys need to come with me to the office now, so I can call your parents."

"Mr. Parrins," says Andrea. "What exactly have we done that's so serious? It's not like we broke windows, or showed up drunk. We just did what we needed to do to get here. To be with our friends."

I feel her reach out and grab my hand. A second later, Sean grabs my other hand. We have become, potentially, the most pitiful human chain in history. At least we're well dressed.

"Please," says Andrea. "Please give us a break. Just this once."

Mr. Parrins glares at us but doesn't say anything. It's all I can do to not start singing "Born This Way."

"Oh for crying out loud," he says finally. "Fine. I'll pretend I didn't see anything. But you still shouldn't be back here. Come with me."

"That was some Jedi mind shit, Andrea," I whisper as we follow Mr. Parrins through a series of empty corridors. He stops at a set of double doors that lead into the gym and uses one of the keys hanging around his neck to unlock it.

"Give me a couple of minutes to get back around to the front," he says. "And don't let me catch you three up to anything shifty once you're in there."

"You won't," says Andrea. "Thanks a million, Mr. Parrins." He's already halfway down the hallway, shaking his head.

I reach for the door handle, but Andrea grabs me by the arm.

"What's wrong?" I ask her.

"Do you think I look stupid?" she asks us.

"You look awesome," I tell her. "Andrea is after a guy," I explain to Sean.

"I can't imagine a straight guy on earth who wouldn't fall for you," he tells her. I swoon internally.

"I just don't think I look like me," she says. "I look like a poser or something."

I put my hand on her shoulder. "Andrea, you look great. It's prom night—everyone is dressed up and partying and dancing. People are too preoccupied with themselves to think anything, except that you look amazing. Tonight is supposed to be fun. Now can we please go in there before I turn into a pumpkin?"

"Thanks, Roemi."Andrea abruptly steps forward and hugs me. Then she turns and hugs Sean.

"Justin won't be able to take his eyes off you," I tell her. "Now let's go. There's less than a half hour left before the lights come on again."

I look at Sean and he looks at me and we both smile.

"Do you feel like dancing?" he asks me.

"What do you think?" I ask, grabbing him by the hand and pulling him through the doors into the gym.

ANDREA

It's surprising how good the gym looks. You could almost forget that you're standing on a basketball court. There are trees spray-painted silver, with little white lights hanging in them, and glowing paper globes hanging from the rafters.

Roemi and Sean immediately head for the packed dance floor. I have no intention of dancing, but when Roemi realizes I haven't followed them, he runs back and grabs my hand, pulling me into the crowd.

I do my best to move around to the music, but I honestly have no experience dancing. Roemi and Sean move in perfect sync, and in world-record time a circle opens up around them. Roemi starts to pull out some incredible moves, and Sean keeps up with him. They begin doing kind of a Russian kick dance with some perfectly executed moonwalks thrown in.

At the breakdown in the middle of the song, people start chanting.

"Go, Roemi, Roemi!"

"OH!" he yells, jumping into the air and kicking his heels together.

"Go, Roemi, Roemi!"

"OH!"

As much as I hate dancing, it's impossible to not be impressed.

I'm cheering and clapping along with everyone else when Bethanne comes squealing up behind me.

"Oh my god!" she screams. "You came! You came!" She takes a step back and sizes me up. "You look amazing!" she says.

"You think so?"

She nods rapidly. "Where did you get this dress?" she asks me.

"Long story," I tell her. "I'll fill you in later."

She leans in to whisper in my ear. "Don't look now," she says, "but you're getting seriously checked out."

I turn and see Justin staring at me. When he realizes I've seen him, he blushes and waves, then scurries away as if he's embarrassed.

"He was asking about you," says Bethanne. "You have to go talk to him!"

"I will," I say. "But I need to make a call first. I'll be right back."

I find a semi-quiet corner in the school foyer. After only two rings, my mom picks up.

"Mom, it's me."

"Andrea, where the hell are you? Are you with your brother? He isn't answering his phone. I told him, there's nothing funny about—"

"Mom!" I say, cutting her off. "I know you're worried about me, and I'm sorry, but I have to tell you something."

"What is it?" she asks, her voice suddenly hushed and worried.

"I want to have fun, Mom. I'm at the prom and I want to stay at the prom and have fun until it's over. I'm not drinking, I'm not on drugs, and I have no intention of getting in a car with anyone who is."

"I'm coming to get you," she says.

"No!" I say. "No, you're not coming to get me. I'm seventeen years old, and there's a boy here that I like, a lot. I know that you're worried about me turning into Brad, but you can stop worrying. I'm going to be fine. I'm not a rule breaker, Mom. I'm never going to be a rule breaker. Okay?"

"Andrea," she says. "You're not making any sense. I don't know what you're talking about."

"I'm just asking you to trust me, Mom. Please?"

There's a long pause on the other end of the line. Then I hear her sigh. "Just a minute," she says.

She must put her hand over the receiver, because I can hear her talking to Dad, but it's all muffled and I can't make out what they're saying. After a few moments she comes back on the line.

"Please be smart, Andrea," she says.

"I always am," I say. "Thanks, Mom. I'll see you tomorrow."

I turn off my phone and go back into the dance. Roemi and Sean, laughing and sweaty from dancing, come rushing over to me.

"Roemi just pointed Justin out to me," says Sean. "He's totally cute."

"I have to admit," says Roemi, "your dream nerd cleans up right nice. Now are you going to talk to him or what?" He points, and I turn to see Justin standing by himself at the edge of the stage. I take a deep breath and move through the crowd toward him. As he sees me approaching, a smile stretches across his face, and he moves to meet me.

"Hey," he says. "You made it."

"Yep," I say. "Despite myself."

He laughs. "Your mom is kind of intense," he says.

"Intensely embarrassing," I say. "I can't believe she actually crashed Terry's party looking for me."

"Everybody's parents are embarrassing," he says. "Anyway, I'm glad you made it. You look really nice."

"Thanks," I say.

We stand there kind of goofily smiling at each other.

The song that's been playing ends and all of a sudden some generic Taylor Swift ballad about princesses and pickup trucks is blasting through the gym. The dance floor thins out; only couples are left, swaying with their arms around each other.

What the hell, I think. "Do you want to dance?" I ask. "Definitely."

I hook my arms around his neck and he puts his around my waist. For a little while neither of us says anything. We just move slowly in a circle.

"Do you think maybe you want to go do something sometime?" he asks suddenly.

"Totally," I tell him. "Like what?"

"I don't know," he says. "I haven't thought that far ahead." I laugh, and he smiles and blushes. Totally cute.

"I'm sure we can figure something out," I say.

The ballad ends and something a lot faster and more upbeat replaces it. I'm not sure I've even heard this song before, but everyone else in the gym freaks out, and the floor is full in just a few minutes. The music is crunchy and pushy and loud, and I'm pretty sure I would hate it if I heard it anywhere else in the world and on any other night. But tonight, I find that I'm actually able to move to the music. My brain has nothing to do with it, and for the moment, I'm happy to let my body take over.

I pull away from Justin and smile at him, lifting an eyebrow and looking at him in a new way, staring directly into those beautiful eyes. He catches my gaze and smiles, blushes and turns away, but only for a second. Soon he's staring right back at me. We're surrounded by what feels like a million people, shaking and jumping like fools, and I'm finally face-to-face with the guy I've been thinking about for so long.

"I usually hate dancing," he yells into my ear.

"Me too!" I yell back, laughing.

"This is fun though!" he hollers.

"Yeah!" I yell. "Something about this just makes me want to tear shit up!"

I reach out and grab his hand, and together we start to lose ourselves in the music. The more we dance, jumping and spinning and letting ourselves go, the more fun I begin to have. I see Bethanne on the edge of the crowd, and I wave for her to come and dance with us. Then Roemi and Sean appear, and the five of us dance in a circle. The whole time, Justin stays right next to me, and I keep catching him stealing looks at me and smiling.

The thing I've never understood about dancing till now is that it only looks stupid when you're on the outside, watching other people do it. When you're part of the crowd, moving along with everyone else, I can't imagine anything else being quite as much fun.

PAUL

"Why'd you help them?" I ask Candace after Andrea and Roemi and Sean have disappeared into the shadows of the school.

"What difference does it make?" she asks.

"It's just kind of funny," I say. "You found Roemi a date. You helped Andrea get ready for the dance. It seems like I'm the only one you haven't helped. Seems like I've been helping you all night, and all I get is a bunch of attitude."

"So what are you saying?" she asks. "You want a rose tattoo too?"

"Nah, I'm cool. I'm just picking on you."

"How about I tell you a story?" she says.

"Why not?" I say.

"You remember when I mentioned that I used to have a boyfriend?" she asks. "But it didn't work out?"

"Yeah," I say.

"His name was Rick. He was older than me. I met him over a year ago, when I'd just turned sixteen and he was almost twenty. I wasn't getting along with my parents very well. Not that I get along great with them now, but it was really bad back then. They were fighting with each other all the time, and I had a serious hate-on for both of them. Especially my mom, because it turned out she'd been cheating on my dad. Anyway, it's a lot more complicated than that, and I don't really want to go into that part of the story."

"Sure," I say, wondering where she's going with this.

"So I was spending a lot of time away from home. When I wasn't at school, I was usually at my friend Vanessa's place, at least at first. When I wasn't with Vanessa, I was out trying to get better at tagging. Like, wandering around with some markers and shit, trying to find places to throw up designs or whatever."

"Kind of like tonight," I say.

"Yeah, but way more Mickey Mouse than that. Kid stuff. I wasn't very good—I was just learning. Then I met Rick. I'd stopped hanging out with Vanessa. She was acting like a narc, telling me I was going to get in trouble or something."

Candace stops and thinks for a few seconds. "Looking back at it now," she says, "I guess maybe I should have listened to her, but I didn't, so what can you do? Anyway, I was out one night, wandering around with a few spray cans in my backpack, looking for a place to practice, and I came across Rick and a couple of his buddies underneath an overpass. His friends tried to get me to leave, but I guess he could tell I was interested in what they were doing, because he got them to back off, and he told me to stick around.

"After that, he kind of took me under his wing. I even started skipping school just to hang out with him and watch him work."

"So that's how you learned," I say.

"That's not all I learned," she says. "Soon he had me helping him break into places to paint. I did everything he asked, because I thought we were a team. It turned out he really just needed a scapegoat, someone to take the heat if the cops showed up. Which might even have happened, if it wasn't for Vanessa."

"What did she do?" I ask her.

"She ratted me out," she says. "I made the mistake of telling her what was going on. I thought she'd understand. She's creative—she's actually a really good artist. But instead of listening to what I was trying to tell her, she got in touch with my mom."

"Whoa," I say.

"Yeah. So my parents basically followed me one night and confronted me with Rick. They told him to stay away from me, and he did. I haven't spoken to him since. Turns out it didn't take much to get him to back off. Obviously it didn't keep me from doing graffiti, but now that Rick's not around, it's pretty much a solo game for me."

"Why do you keep doing it?" I ask her.

"Because it's who I am," she says. "I don't mean breaking into places and stuff like that, just the art. I guess that's what I'm trying to tell you. You should be honest about who you are. To everyone. It isn't fair to keep your girlfriend in the dark."

She reaches out and punches me in the arm. "How could she not love who you really are?"

I don't say anything. I just turn and stare toward the school. The only sound is the distant bass throbbing from the sound system in the gym.

* * *

When I get to the school, the front doors are locked, as I knew they would be. I can see a bunch of teachers standing around inside the main entry, gossiping and probably flirting with each other. I hammer on the door a few times to get their attention. It works. They stop talking and turn to stare at me.

Mr. Chan, the vice-principal, shakes his head at me and points to his watch, but I bang on the door again and keep at it until he comes and unlocks it from the inside.

"Paul," he says, opening the door a crack and speaking to me from inside, "you know you can't come inside this late. The doors are closed. Not to mention you're wearing jeans. There's a dress code, you know."

"I'm not here for the prom, Mr. Chan," I tell him. "I need to talk to Alannah Freston. It's important."

"I'm sorry, Paul," he says. "You'll have to wait until the dance is over."

"Mr. Chan," I say, looking him straight in the eye, "I need to talk to Lannie now. It's important."

He gives me a funny look, as if he's trying to decide how serious I am, then pushes the door open and lets me through.

"You've got ten minutes before I come in and find you," he says. "That's it."

"Thanks," I say, walking past the cluster of curious teachers and through the doors to the gym.

I stand there for a minute and look around. It takes awhile for my eyes to adjust to the dimness. I spot Jerry and Ahmed with their dates.

"Holy shit, man," says Ahmed when I walk up to them. "What are you doing here?"

"People were saying you were in the hospital with pneumonia," says Jerry. "Then Penner showed up and started spreading some story about you and Roemi hanging out with some satan-worshipping chick. It didn't make much sense, but he's pretty messed up."

"None of that is exactly true," I say. "Listen, I only have a minute, but I was wondering if you guys want to come over to my place tomorrow. Shoot some hoops or something?"

They exchange quick glances. I can't really blame them for being suspicious.

"Are you sure, man?" asks Jerry. "You don't have something else going on with Lannie?"

"Nah," I say. "I'd rather hang out with you guys. No worries if you're busy or whatever."

"No, man, that sounds cool," says Ahmed. "We'll be over."

"Awesome," I say. "By the way, have any of you seen Lannie?"

"Yeah," says Jerry. "She's been hanging out in the corner of the gym all night."

Darrah spots me first. She leans in to whisper to Lannie, who turns around to face me as I approach.

Even with her arms crossed, not smiling, Lannie is incredibly hot. Hot and definitely unimpressed.

"Look who showed up," says Penner. "Where's your boyfriend anyway, York?" he asks.

"Give it a rest, Penner," I tell him. I turn to Lannie. "Hey," I say. "I've been looking for you."

"What are you doing here?" she asks. "I spent all night worrying about you, and then Ryan told me that you aren't sick after all."

"I know, Lannie," I say. "I'm really sorry. I owe you an apology."

"Can you please just tell me what's going on?"

"Come on," Darrah says to Penner. "Let's dance." She drags him away.

"It feels kind of weird to say this out loud, " I say.

"Just spit it out."

"When I was a kid," I say, "I used to have panic attacks. Bad ones. I had to go to therapy, and eventually I got over them. But this week I started having them again. I don't know why, but every time I thought about coming here, to prom, they got worse. So when you talked to my mom this morning, that's what was happening. I was in the middle of a really bad panic attack."

Lannie just stares at me. Then she bursts out laughing.

"What's so funny?" I ask her.

"Sorry," she says. "I thought you were going to break up with me or something. Panic attacks? Really?" She starts to laugh again.

"Yeah," I say. "Really. They're kind of hard to describe. I get dizzy, my heart races, and my mind fills up with crazy thoughts. They're pretty intense."

She waves me off. "Please," she says. "I know what it's like to freak out about exams or a game or whatever."

"It's not really the same thing," I say.

"Well, whatever it is," she says, "it doesn't explain why you ended up hanging out with Roemi Kapoor and some strange girl."

"Well, it's kind of a funny story."

"I bet it is," she says. "I don't really want to hear it right now. My night has been ruined enough already."

"I'm really sorry," I tell her again. "You look incredible."

She manages a half smile. "Thanks," she says. She closes her eyes and exhales deeply. "Listen," she says. "Do you want to get out of here? Go get something to eat? We can grab Darrah and Ryan and maybe go to Bizzby's."

"I don't really feel like hanging out with Penner right now," I tell her. "He was kind of an asshole when he ran into me before."

"You know what he's like," she says.

"What if we went with some other people instead?" I ask her.

She raises an eyebrow at me. "What other people?"

"Roemi and his date, Sean," I say. "Andrea and Justin. Maybe Jerry and Ahmed."

"Andrea Feingold?" she asks. "Jerry and Ahmed? Roemi? Are you nuts?"

"They're my friends, Lannie," I say.

"Well, they're not mine," she says. "Come on. Let's just go by ourselves. Darrah and Ryan can do their own thing."

She reaches out and grabs my hand. I look down at her freshly manicured fingers, the smooth pale skin on her wrist. My eyes trace a line up her bare arm, along her neck, up to her perfect face, staring at me, waiting for me to follow her anywhere she wants. I pull away from her.

"Do you know what, Lannie?" I say. "I don't think it's going to work out between us."

Her mouth drops open.

"Let's face it," I go on. "As soon as you graduate and get to college, you're just going to dump me for someone who does a better job of living up to your expectations. Why waste the time?"

"Okay, hang on," she says. "*You* don't break up with *me*. I should be the one breaking up with you." On the surface she sounds confident, as if she's still in control of the situation, but I can tell that she's panicking. I actually feel sorry for her. Lannie Freston isn't used to people telling her she can't have what she wants.

"Okay then, Lannie," I say. "Feel free. Break up with me."

She doesn't say anything for a moment. She just stands there as the confusion on her face turns to anger.

"Screw you, Paul," she says finally. Then she turns and storms away.

I'm heading for the exit when the lights come on, throwing a harsh glare down into the gym. There's a collective groan and some jeers and boos, and the music comes to an abrupt end. I get caught up in the crowd as everyone beelines for the front doors at the same time. Somebody grabs my arm, and I turn to see Roemi, huddled with Sean, Andrea, Justin and Bethanne.

"What's going on?" he asks. "Why are you here?"

"I decided that I needed to talk to Lannie," I tell them.

"Did you find her?" Andrea asks.

"Yeah," I say.

"And you're leaving by yourself," says Roemi. "So does this mean…?"

"Yeah," I say. "We broke up."

"Thank god," he says. "I was wondering if one of us was going to have to do it for you."

"Roemi!" says Andrea.

"What?" he says. "Am I wrong?"

We squeeze through the bottleneck at the front doors. Once we're outside, the six of us move down the sidewalk, away from the crowd and off to the side.

"My parents are parked down the street," says Bethanne. "Do you want a ride home, Andrea?"

Andrea glances at Justin, who smiles at her. "I think I'm okay," she says. "I'll make it home all right."

"Okay," says Bethanne. "See you later, guys! Bye, Paul," she says, looking right at me and smiling before she hurries away.

"Brace yourself, Paul," says Roemi. "You're going to be drowning in women once they hear that you dumped Lannie."

"Hey!" someone yells. "York!"

I turn and look down the sidewalk. Penner is pointing at me. Lannie and Darrah are standing right behind him, staring at us.

"This guy sure knows how to make an entrance," says Roemi as Penner strides toward us.

"What do you want, Ryan?" I ask.

"What do you want?" he repeats, mocking me. "Are you seriously dumping the hottest girl in school to hang out with a bunch of losers and homos?"

A crowd starts to gather around us, people whispering to each other. I notice Jerry and Ahmed have pushed their way to the front.

"What do you care?" I ask him. "And quit talking shit about my friends, Penner. Take it back."

"Oh, I'm sorry," he says. "I meant to say *faggots*, not *homos*."

"Whoa," says Sean, moving to stand next to me. "Who are you calling a faggot?"

"Who are you?" asks Penner.

"I'm Roemi's date," says Sean. "Not that it's any of your business."

"Well, I guess I'm calling you a faggot then," says Penner. He takes a step forward. Out of the corner of my eye, I see Jerry take his jacket off and hand it to his date, and he and Ahmed move a bit closer to us.

Darrah pushes through the crowd and grabs Penner by the arm. "Come on, Ryan," she says.

"Get out of my way," he says. He shakes her off with his arm, and she stumbles backward. She stares at him for a moment with her mouth open, then starts to cry and runs back to Lannie.

Penner is a big guy, but it occurs to me that he's totally outmanned. Sean is standing his ground right next to me, and I know that Jerry and Ahmed are ready to jump in if things escalate. The last thing I want is to get caught up in a fight, but I'm facing off against Penner whether I like it or not.

"That's enough!" I hear Roemi yell from behind me. He shoves his way between me and Sean and walks right up to Penner.

"Listen here, you two-bit, knuckle-dragging, shit-for-brains orangutan," he says, standing on his tiptoes and getting his face right up into Penner's. "Nobody in this school likes you. Nobody in this town respects you. Nobody on earth thinks you're funny or intelligent or attractive, with the exception of your girlfriend and possibly your mom, and the jury's still out on her. So why don't you back off and leave me and my friends alone?"

Penner's eyes widen and his jaw clenches, and you can practically see the veins in his forehead pop. He leans in toward Roemi so that their noses are almost touching, but Roemi doesn't flinch. A hush falls over the crowd, and the moment seems to drag on forever. Then Penner steps back, gives Roemi the finger and turns to walk away.

"That's right," Roemi calls after him. "Don't let the door hit you on the ass."

Penner stops in his tracks and stiffens. He turns around, glaring, and charges at Roemi. It all happens so quickly that before anyone has a chance to intervene, it's already over. There's a blur of activity, and somehow Penner gets flipped onto the ground and Roemi ends up sitting on his back with one of Penner's arms twisted back in an unnatural position.

"Say uncle," says Roemi. Penner wriggles and tries to get up, but every time he moves, Roemi twists harder. "Say uncle!" Roemi yells again.

"Uncle," comes Penner's muffled reply.

Roemi gets up and steps back, and Penner scrambles to his feet. He stands there for a minute, confused and disoriented, and then stumbles over to Darrah.

"Come on," he says. "We're going."

"Whatever," she says. "We're through, Ryan."

He looks as if he wants to say something else, but instead he shoves his way through the crowd. When he gets to the street, he starts running.

"What the hell just happened?" asks Andrea.

Roemi shrugs. "I guess seven years of martial-arts training was worth every penny." He walks over to Sean, reaches out and grabs him by the waist, and pulls him in for a long, lingering kiss. The crowd cheers and hollers and then Roemi steps back, turns to where Andrea and Justin and I are standing and does a three-phase finger snap in the air.

"Let's roll, bitches," he says, before turning and strutting off toward the Audi.

CANDACE

After Paul heads to the school to work things out with Lannie, I sit on the hood of the car for a while, just thinking. It's been a better night than I ever would have expected, and I can't help feeling a bit of karmic satisfaction about the way things have turned out. Paul is making up with his girlfriend. Roemi finally has a date. Andrea is at the prom after all, and if I do say so myself, she looks great.

There's just one more thing to take care of.

I stare at my phone for a long time before making the call. After the third ring, I start to second-guess myself, and I'm about to press End when I hear someone pick up.

"Candace?" I hear Vanessa say. There's a lot of background noise, and I can barely make her out.

"Hey, Vanessa," I say.

"Hang on a sec," she says. "I'm going somewhere quieter."

In a minute I can hear her clearly.

"Hey," she says. "Sorry about that. A few of us came to Bizzby's after the dance. I'm in the parking lot."

"How was prom?" I ask.

"It was okay," she says. "You know what that shit is like."

"Looked like you were having a good time with Evan," I say.

She laughs. "Yeah," she says. "We've been hanging out lately."

"I'm happy for you," I say.

"Thanks," she says.

I hesitate. I'm sure she's wondering why I'm calling, but I'm not sure how to put it into words.

"Listen," I finally say. "I'm really sorry."

"No," she says. "I'm sorry. I know I've said it already, but I'm really, really sorry. I should never have talked to your parents."

"You were just being a good friend," I say. "I don't blame you. I mean, I did blame you, but I shouldn't have." I'm embarrassed to feel my eyes start to sting.

I feel tears rolling down my face, and my nose starts to run. I try to sniff and end up choking, and that makes me laugh.

"Are you okay?" she asks.

"Yeah," I say. "I'm fine. Listen, what are you doing tomorrow night?"

"No plans," she says.

"Do you want to come to Granite Ridge and have supper at my gee-ma's place?"

"I'd love to," she says. "I'm there."

"Cool," I say. "So I guess I'll text you tomorrow with details?"

"Perfect," she says. "And Candace?"

"Yeah."

"I'm really happy you called."

"Me too," I say.

When I hang up, I sit for a while, staring across the field at the school. I'm sure the dance will be ending soon, but I know that my night is already over, and it couldn't have ended any better than this. There's really no good reason to stick around waiting for them to come back, so I get up and start walking home.

Just to be safe, I take the quietest, most obscure route I can think of, but when I'm about a block away from Gee-ma's house, I find myself illuminated by the flashing colored lights of the cop cruiser. Of course. I slump my shoulders and turn around as it pulls to a stop next to me.

The cop gets out of the car.

"Boy oh boy," he says. "You just don't know when to quit, do you?"

I don't say anything.

"I see you've still got your backpack," he says. "Why don't you show me what's inside?"

"I don't have to show you anything," I say.

"I beg to differ," he says. "I've got more than enough reason to legally search your bag."

I don't stand a chance. Besides, as much as I hate to admit it, it's not like I'm totally innocent. I sigh and drop my backpack in front of me. I'm bending over to unzip it when the cop's radio crackles on.

We just got a call from someone who lives across the street from Granite Ridge High, says the dispatcher. *She says it looks like a brawl might be in the works. Can someone get over there and break things up?*

The cop looks at me and my pack, then back at the radio.

"You've got nine lives, young lady. Do you understand that?" he says.

I nod.

"Now get your butt home and understand something else. I'll be watching out for you. Don't think I won't remember your face."

He gets back in the car, rolls up his window, puts on his lights and does a U-turn in the middle of the street. I take a deep breath and start to hustle back to Gee-ma's house.

I'm on her street but still a block away when I see the Audi parked against the curb outside her house. Paul and Roemi and Andrea and Sean are leaning against the side of the car along with some other guy I've never seen before.

"What are you guys doing here?" I ask them when I get there.

"You didn't really think we were going to finish off the night without you, did you?" asks Roemi.

"Candace," says Andrea, "this is Justin."

"Hey," I say.

"*The* Justin," says Roemi.

"God, Roemi," says Andrea. "Really?"

"Justin doesn't mind," says Roemi. "Do you mind, Justin?"

"Uh, no," he says, blushing.

Andrea turns to look at him. "Do you want to walk me home?" she says.

"For sure," he says.

"We can give you guys a ride," says Paul.

"Thanks," says Andrea. "But I think we're cool."

"You've got that right," says Roemi. "Cool as ice."

"It's been quite a night," says Andrea. "Thanks to you guys."

"Last day of school Monday," says Paul. "You wanna walk with me, Andrea?"

"Definitely," she says. She looks at me. "We should hang out sometime," she says.

"It's a plan," I say.

When they're halfway down Gee-ma's block, Andrea turns to wave at us. Then she reaches out and takes Justin's hand, and they walk away into the night.

"Roemi and I are about to drive Sean back to the city," says Paul. "You in?"

"Why not?" I say. In case my luck is about to run out, I leave my backpack in the front porch at Gee-ma's house. When I get back to the car, Roemi and Sean are in the backseat together, so I grab shotgun.

Nobody has much to say during the drive. Roemi and Sean are quiet in the backseat, and Paul seems a bit distracted. I'm content to stare out at the approaching lights of the city.

When we get to Sean's building, Roemi gets out to walk him to the front door.

"So I broke up with Lannie," says Paul once we're alone in the car.

"I kind of figured something like that must have happened," I say. "Otherwise, why would you be here right now?"

"Yeah," he says, "why *would* I be here?"

Then he's leaning in toward me. I'm not sure if I've been expecting it or not, but what matters is that in the brief moment when he leans in to kiss me, a lot of shit goes through my head. What do I have in common with this guy? Nothing? Everything? The way people dress and the way their brains operate don't always have a lot to do with each other. People are more than their exteriors.

In the end, I decide not to overthink it. Seventeen is too young to know anything about the future. I know there's probably no way in hell that Paul and I make any sense as a couple. I also know that the way I see myself, and the way I see other people, is capable of changing a lot, even over the course of just one night.

How hard can it hurt to give people a chance once in a while?

ROEMI

Best. Prom. Ever.

A few short hours ago, I was the sole occupant of self-pity city. Now look at me. Not only did I break into the school, own the dance floor and take down the king of the troglodytes, I also managed to make some new friends along the way.

Best of all, I finally got the guy. Maybe he wasn't the guy I started out trying to catch, but I think we can all agree that this is the best outcome. Just imagine if John had showed up in the first place. We probably would have had a good time, we might even have made a bit of a splash, but it wouldn't have held a candle to what did happen. And I wouldn't have met Sean.

Driving back to the city, nobody says much. I keep sneaking peeks at Sean, wondering what he's thinking.

Was the kiss just a fluke? Did I catch him so off-guard that he didn't have time to back away? Is tonight just a one-time thing, a favor for Candace?

We pull up in front of his house, and I get out to walk with him to his front door. He turns and smiles at me. I want to reach out and grab him by the hand, but I can't build up the nerve.

"Thanks for coming on such short notice," I say. I immediately want to smash myself in the head. *Such short notice?*

"I had a really great time," he says.

"Seriously," I say. "I don't know if you understand how awesome it was to actually have a date tonight."

"I hope it was even more important to have the right date," he says.

"Of course," I say, my heart pounding. "Are we ever going to see each other again?"

"Are you kidding?" he asks, laughing. "It's not like we live that far away from each other."

"No," I say. "I mean, do you want to see me again?"

He leans in and starts kissing me, soft but insistent.

"What do you think?" he asks when he pulls away.

"I'm at a loss for words," I say. "This might be a first."

"That's all right," he says. "We've got plenty of time to figure out the right things to say."

We make out for a while, pressed against the side of his house.

"I should go," I say finally. "I'll call you tomorrow?"

"I'll be waiting," he says, winking at me before going inside.

I collapse into the backseat of the car, and Paul and Candace turn around to look at me, laughing.

"Looks like I was right about you guys hitting it off," says Candace.

"Candace," I say, "you are officially my favorite person in the world right now."

"That's great," she says.

I sit up and lean between the front seats, which is when I notice that Paul's hand is on Candace's leg.

"What the hell is going on?" I ask. They look at each other and burst out laughing again.

"What do you think?" asks Paul.

"Jesus," I say. "Was there Spanish fly in our Starbucks? Are you guys…what are you guys…?"

"Why so eager to define everything, Roemi?" asks Candace.

"Yeah yeah," I say. "I get it. But I want to be on record as saying that this is as weird as it gets. Weird in a good way, of course. You have my blessing, you crazy kids. Now can we go home? I'm exhausted."

After dropping Candace off, which involves a brief delay for some jock-on-goth action, Paul finally pulls the Audi into my driveway. We get out and he hands me the keys.

"Tell your dad how awesome it was that he let me drive his car," he says.

"For sure," I say. "I guarantee that if you're willing to stop by for ice cream and car talk with him once in a while, he'll let you take it out again. I get shotgun though."

"Of course."

"You don't mind walking home?" I say. "I could wake Dad up to drive you."

"No, man," he says. "It's totally cool. A walk will be good right about now."

"Well, I guess this is it," I say. "Prom night is officially over."

"Yup," he says.

"Thanks for driving us around all night."

"It was cool, man," he says. "It was fun to hang out."

"Oddly enough," I say.

"Yeah, well." He smiles.

I reach out and he grabs my hand and gives it a solid shake, then pulls me in and gives me a one-armed hug and a slap on the back, the way you see football players do it. "Peace, man," he says.

"You got it," I say.

I watch as he walks away. At the bottom of my driveway he turns around.

"Hey, Roemi," he calls. "We should hang out again sometime. I'll text you."

"You better," I call back.

He shoves his hands in his pockets and starts to whistle as he disappears down the street.

I let myself into the house and make it up to my room without waking up my parents. I stand in front of the mirror and take one last look at myself in the tuxedo before taking it off and hanging it up in my closet. I'm brushing my teeth when I hear my phone ding.

It's a text from Sean.

Thinking about you, it says.

What a coincidence, I write back.

I climb into bed and lie there for a while, wide awake.

In the end, I wasn't part of the first gay couple to ever attend a GRHS prom (I'll see you in hell, Allison Jackson), but in the long run, that doesn't really matter. Life isn't about being the first, or doing the best, or having the most. It's about shaking things up, taking some chances, getting to know new people.

I have no idea what's going to happen to any of us. Who does?

But I do know this. Next time I need to take care of some business, I know some people who might be willing to tag along with me.

And I'm pretty sure we'll be ready to go off-script, if necessary.

ACKNOWLEDGMENTS

Thank you to my family and friends for their love and encouragement. Thanks to the gang at Orca for working so hard on all of my books. Special thanks to my editor, Sarah Harvey, for her friendship and great advice. Thank you so much to the wonderful Robin Stevenson for reading an early draft of the story and giving me some great feedback. Thanks to my old buddy, Graeme Hopkins, for helping me understand cars a little bit better. Thanks to the Apocalypsies for being such an incredible support network and mutual appreciation society. Finally, thank you to Andrew for being the very best in every way.

Tom Ryan was born and raised in Inverness, on Cape Breton Island. Like most transplanted Cape Bretoners, he spends a lot of time wishing he was back on the right side of the causeway. He currently lives in Ottawa, Ontario, with his partner and dog. He can be found online at www.tomwrotethat.com.